A IS FOR AMOUR

EROTIC STORIES
EDITED BY ALISON TYLER

CLEIS
PRESS

Published in the United States by Cleis Press Inc.,
P.O. Box 14697, San Francisco, California 94114.

Printed in the United States.
Cover design: Scott Idleman
Text design: Karen Quigg
Cleis Press logo art: Juana Alicia
First Edition.
10 9 8 7 6 5 4 3 2 1

A IS FOR AMOUR

Also by Alison Tyler

———

Acknowledgments

Appreciative Applause goes to:

Adam Nevill

Barbara Pizio

Felice Newman

Frédérique Delacoste

Diane Levinson

Violet Blue

and SAM, always.

Love is a smoke made with the fume of sighs.
Being purged, a fire sparkling in lovers' eyes.
Being vexed, a sea nourished with lovers' tears.
What is it else?
A madness most discreet, a choking gall and a preserving sweet.

—WILLIAM SHAKESPEARE

Why won't you ever know that I'm in love with you?
That I'm in love with you?

—THE CURE

contents

INTRODUCTION

All you need is love.
Love is a many splendored thing.
Love makes the world go 'round.

A LL RIGHT. So all of those statements are true. And yet none even begin to describe what love truly is. *Love* is simply one of those words that means entirely different things to different people. I've known this for years. Anyone who listens to rock 'n' roll as obsessively as I do understands that love is a contradiction all by itself—elusive, fleeting, transitory, all-consuming, endless, explosive, unavoidable, and necessary.

Still, when I put out a call for submissions with the vague theme of "Amour," I found myself surprised by the range of love affairs that writers conjured. From Tsaurah Litzky's "Sharing the Love," which deals with a risqué three-way between two committed partners and their longtime friend to Jolene Hui's "Parker's Mustache," which focuses on a love of facial hair (facial hair belonging to the narrator's brother-in-law), these creative authors showed me the love in completely unexpected ways.

Love is longing in Saskia Walker's "Arran's Lure": "'Face it, girl, you've got it bad,'" she murmured…. And the worst of it was that it hurt. Hurt bad. Being in love was a screwed-up painful thing, if you were apart from the one you loved."

Love is lust in Radclyffe's "All about Us": "When I skimmed her nipples, already puckered and hard, she moaned and jacked me faster.

"'You don't want to do that so hard, baby,' I warned breathlessly. 'Not unless you want me to come in my pants right now.'"

Love is blind, blind enough to make Cleveland seem like Paris, as in *"Le Petit Déjeuner"* by Jeremy Edwards: "When no one is looking, we refer to the immediate neighborhood as the *arrondissement*. The bookshelves are sprinkled with Balzac and *Asterix*. Unassuming Rhône wines haunt the kitchen counter, echoing the mood of the lazy still life that freshens the living room with flowers and peaches."

These stories approach love from all angles. The downside. The upside. The wanting so bad you can't sleep. Which is when *A Is for Amour* comes in handy. Flick on your bedside lamp. Crack the spine. And get ready to fall in love.

XXX,
Alison Tyler

Saskia Walker

Arran's Lure

ALONE IN HER BED, Juliet lay with her sheets twisted between her arms and legs, thinking about Christopher. Wanting him. Craving him. There was a point where her physical desire for him had turned into an all-consuming hunger. Since then, she had been continually restless with need. Finding sleep was no longer easy. The longing she felt for that one person whose shared passion would provide her lifeline, her relief, had long since become overwhelming.

"Christopher Bardsley, what on earth have you done to me?" she whispered into the night, and a smile passed over her lips.

She felt high at times, at others wretched. Her fierce physical desire also manifested itself in a painful, gnawing ache that emanated out from between her thighs, through her core, as far as her throat and mind, where she was tortured with memory and longing. Her fingers tightened on her rumpled sheets, as did her thighs, her body rolling restlessly.

Masturbation just left her hungry for what she couldn't have, a particularly cruel twist of fate. She needed to express herself to him, to join their bodies together again. And he was so far away. Over four hundred miles, to be precise. It might as well have been ten thousand, the way she felt.

She was at home in London, trying unsuccessfully to focus on her freelance journalism—her one and only love before she met him—and he was off the coast of Scotland, on the Isle of Arran. That's where she'd met him, interviewing him as part of a series of features on unusual people who had forced their careers to fit their lives, instead of allowing the opposite to happen.

Christopher owned and ran a major Internet provisions company. He'd built it up from nothing, but when he'd inherited his uncle's farming land in the south of Arran, he'd decided to up sticks and move there. He managed his Internet company from an entirely different kind of base, in order to maintain the traditions of his family line, making both aspects of his life work.

Juliet had traveled up by train and ferry to meet him, and found herself stunned by the beauty of Arran, even as she looked at it from the windswept ferry on the approach to the port of Brodick. It was this landscape that had motivated his monumental move, his choice to oversee the farm, meshing a long-standing farming lifestyle with that of a modern day businessman.

"I came to look at the place, and I experienced the lure of the island. I'd visited as a child, and I had very fond memories of the farm, but as an adult who has traveled the world, it just took hold of me." He observed her as he spoke, turning a heavy tumbler in his hand, warming the rich local malt whisky it contained.

She nodded, feeling the place and its master instill their lure in her, too. Sitting opposite him on the sofa, sipping the fine scotch, her desire ran rampant. From his hand nursing the glass, to the strong outline of his thighs through his black jeans, he drew her attention in every way. Desire thrummed in her every pulse point, her blood racing, her lips eager to brush against the firm line of his mouth.

As soon as she saw him, she wanted him. He said it was the same for him, too. She'd booked into a B&B, but never spent a single night there. Arriving at his house, she saw him in action, instructing the land workers for the following day, answering a call from Denmark in the next moment.

"What drives you?" she asked, later that evening, as they sat in his comfortable sitting room after a dinner prepared by his housekeeper. It was a question she'd asked all the men and women she had interviewed for the series.

"The need to make the impossible work." He paused, and the corners of his mouth lifted in an insinuating smile. "What drives you?"

No one had ever turned the question on her before, and it wasn't something she had ever thought about, but still she knew the answer. "The need to express myself, I guess."

He nodded. "I've read your work; you express yourself well. I'd like to see more than that, though." His gray-green eyes twinkled. He asked her questions, found out things she didn't even know about herself.

"Are you interviewing me now?"

He smiled. "Kind of." He looked her over with an unambiguous stare. "I'm sure I could find you an appropriate position." The expression he wore was filled with raw, uncompromising sexuality, that aspect of his personality just as forthright as every other.

She gave a soft laugh. "I'm sure you could." They both knew it was going to happen, but they talked on, savoring the rich sense of anticipation that built between them.

What was it about him?

She'd never met a man so intensely male, that was for sure. There was an inbuilt sense of power about him, and yet he wasn't blatant or egotistical. It was a calm, self-assured way that he had. He wasn't classically handsome, either. His dark hair was unruly, his body built large and strong. He'd had a rough childhood, but that only seemed to make him steadfast and sure of what he wanted in life. She ached to have him over her, to feel him thrusting into her.

"What's life without a few risks," he commented, and she knew he wasn't just talking about business ventures. He put his glass down and reached out to touch her face.

She'd never been shy about letting a man know what she wanted. "I'm right with you on that one." She turned her face into the palm of his hand, kissing it, opening her mouth to taste his skin.

Their kisses were raw, needy, while they stripped each other with eager hands. The first time was hard and fast, right there on the rug in front of the log fire. She welcomed the hard strength his body, hungry for it, her cunt hot and grabbing, holding him tight as he pulled back and lunged. As they got closer to the climax, he raised up on his arms, looking down at her with searching eyes, and she latched her legs over his shoulders, sucking him ever deeper. The climax hit her in a dizzy, wild rush, and he followed fast, one hand pressing her pubic bone down onto his cock, the pressure releasing a second wave of pleasure through her.

Her fingers knotted in his hair when he lay over her, holding him close. Something unstoppable had been set in motion between them. He'd kissed and touched her everywhere, before he carried her to his bed and fucked her again, slowly, taking shallow strides, making her mad for it. He laughed softly when she begged him for more, looking at her in the light that spilled in through the large picture window. The sound of the waves crashing against the cliffs was all that had anchored her to the reality of the moment, when he drove the length of his cock inside her, filling her to overfull.

She'd phoned the agency, called in sick, something she'd never done before, lengthening her stay on the island, lengthening her time with him.

"Tell me now, what do you want?" he said against her ear, whilst he screwed her from behind.

"I want it to last and last," she'd cried out, poised on the edge of her orgasm. "I want to feel your cock right through me." Moaning loudly, she drove back onto him, spilling down her thighs as she came. He'd pulled out, pacing himself when he got too close, giving her exactly what she wanted. He possessed her over again, until she could barely move and her cunt was blissfully sore, riotous with sensation from fucking, her mind and body senseless with multiple, rolling orgasms. When she collapsed on the bed, he knelt over her, taking his cock in his hand. She caught sight of the pent-up ecstasy and pain of his held-back release in his expression. In that moment she saw it all: this was a man who got what he wanted, who worked for it, no matter how hard, no matter what the sacrifice. He came over her belly. Panting hard, he bent over her, rubbing his semen over her breasts and torso.

"Yes, yes," she begged, "stain me, mark me."

His expression was fiercely possessive as he marked his territory, the ritualized action making her feel gloriously proud as she lay sated in his arms.

They barely slept, afraid to waste the precious time together. Instead they fucked hard, then made love slow. They lay awake in the moonlight communicating with mouths, fingers, and tongues. They explored each other almost continually, talking endlessly, then rolling together, his mouth on her pussy and hers on his cock, devouring each other.

"Why did you come here?" he whispered with a dark smile, one night, in the midst of their passion.

"I'm not so sure anymore," she replied, joyous laughter escaping her mouth.

She'd never expressed herself so thoroughly, giving everything, opening herself in ways that she hadn't even considered possible. He confessed he was stubbornly independent, and she knew that alone made this hard for him. She recognized that was why he was alone. Too focused for his own good.

In the daytime, he drove her across the island to the rougher landscape of the north, where he took her down to the cliffs. The blustery autumnal winds nudged them up against shoreline. Their words and laughter were lifted on the whirling wind around their heads before disappearing.

"Come here, I have to be inside you now," he'd said, and backed her against the cliff wall. He opened her coat and lifted her skirt, his hands moving fast into the heat of her. Over his shoulder she saw that the tide was coming in, the waves rolling over the sand in the timeless embrace between land and sea.

"Now?" she replied, weak with desire, emotion catching in her throat.

He answered by stripping her underwear down her legs, knocking off one shoe and lifting one leg in his hand, before plunging deep inside her.

She was acutely aware of the rough rock at her back as he rode her against the ancient cliff face, lifting her bodily with each thrust. "The tide is coming in," she cried, her hands around his head.

"There's enough time," he replied, hoarsely, and she gave in to his overwhelming need.

She'd never been fucked the way he fucked her, like he was claiming her to the core, to the very soul. And now, lying alone in her bed in London, it was driving her slowly insane with need.

Now.

I want that now.

Flinging the sheet away, she got up and pulled on a T-shirt. Uselessly, she wandered to her desk, where she nudged the mouse. The screen flickered into life as she sat down. There was an email from the main news agency she took assignments from. She'd been ignoring it all day. They were asking if she'd finished the Arran article yet, and if they could have the title, ASAP.

Sighing, she clicked over to the unfinished document. At first, she told herself that when she finished up the article, she'd get over it. Only then would the pain and the intense desire begin to fade. Then, as she found how hard it was to finish, she realized she didn't actually want to, because she didn't want to break that connection with Christopher.

"Face it, girl, you've got it bad," she murmured, as she looked over the copy. And the worst of it was that it hurt. Hurt bad. Being in love was a screwed-up painful thing, if you were apart from the one you loved.

Her phone bleeped into life. Picking it up, her spirits lifted and she smiled at the name on the screen.

"I didn't wake you did I?" His voice.

"Hey you," she said. "Nope. I can't sleep. Thinking about you."

He gave a soft growl. "Good."

"I can hear the sea. Where are you?"

"In the bedroom, standing by the window, looking at the empty bed, wishing you were in it."

"Wanting to make the impossible work?" she teased.

"With a fury."

His tone had a low intensity about it that melted her. She bit her lip, her head dropping back. She could just picture him. Reaching over, she flicked her monitor off, allowing the enveloping darkness to take over. If he were by the window in his bedroom, the moonlight would be at his back. In her mind's eye, she touched his outline, reaching out for him with every atom of her body. Between her thighs she was hot and wet, her inner flesh clutching rhythmically, wanting him there.

"Touch yourself, now," he instructed.

The pulse in her groin beat wildly in response to his words. Her free hand moved between her thighs, her fingers dipping into her well of slick heat, the palm of her hand crushing her clit.

"Do you want me there?" His tone was demanding, almost desperate.

"Oh, yes."

"Make yourself come, let me hear you."

She put one foot up on the edge of the desk, opening her legs wide. He was breathing close to the mouthpiece, and the sound fueled her.

"Describe it, tell me how it feels."

"I'm swollen, I've been thinking of you all evening. My clit is hard, so sensitive." Almost too sensitive, it stung as she flicked it. "Oh God."

"Come, please...let me hear you."

She moved her hand, her cunt locking on one hard finger, hips moving back and forth, palm rocking against her clit. Her moan of release was long and breathless.

"I wish I was there."

She laughed breathlessly. "So do I, believe me."

"It's not getting any easier, is it?" he commented, with a dry laugh.

"No," she agreed. "I'm going to finish the article tonight," she whispered, before she said good-bye.

"That's bad isn't it?"

She couldn't help smiling. He knew that she had been dragging her heels. How had he come to know her so well? A feeling of destiny surrounded her. "No. It doesn't have to be a bad thing. I'm not going to let it be a bad thing, Christopher." In the moment of silence, she sensed his relief.

"Remember what I said."

Her heart brimmed. On their last night together they had lain silently in each other's arms, talking whilst barely speaking, drinking each other in through their eyes. When dawn broke through, he'd fed her breakfast in bed before taking her out to walk across the land. On the hilltop, there was an early morning mist that seemed to hold them to the ground they stood upon. He told her then that he wanted her to come back, that he'd be there for her. Deep inside, she already knew that. She put her fingers to his lips and sank into his embrace, wishing they could stay shrouded in the mist forever. Far too soon, the midmorning sun broke through and it was time for her to catch the ferry to the mainland.

"I remember everything you said," she whispered into the phone. "And you're right. You always were. What's life without a few risks? I want to be with you."

"In that case, I'll move back to London."

For a moment, she was stunned. "No way. You belong there." She paused. "Christopher, trust me, *I* can make the impossible work, too."

"Yes…?"

It was the first time she had ever heard any hint of vulnerability in his voice, and that told her everything she needed to know.

"Yes, love. You've made me braver."

When they finally said good-bye, she poured herself the last measure of Arran malt from the bottle Christopher had hidden in her overnight bag when she left, and sipped it slowly, savoring its rich, full-bodied taste. Switching on her monitor, she typed a letter to the agencies she worked for, informing them of her upcoming change of location, flagging up her availability for assignments in Scotland and the north.

Turning to the article, she rubbed her hands together and added her conclusion. Despite her earlier unwillingness, it took her only moments to complete the article. Now that the decision had been made, everything fell into place. Finally, she scrolled to the top, smiling to herself, and added the title: *Arran's Lure: making the impossible scenario work, despite the odds.*

TENILLE BROWN

STRINGS

for John

A NOTE.

That was what would pass for good-bye. She left notes now instead of slipping out while he was sleeping, leaving his apartment in the middle of the night without a word.

That had been her thing for a while, leaving immediately after, not assuming she was staying the night, not waiting for him to ask if she would. She'd had to work up to it, admittedly, five years of marriage had her set in her ways; being on her own again, she'd had to teach herself the ropes.

Love them and leave them alone.

It was her mantra, her new way of life.

The note was polite if nothing else, and the two of them were that to each other: respectful, polite.

Yet it did seem distant somehow, even cold, considering. He had spent the last few hours inside her, after all, but what else could she do? Wake him and thank him for a nice evening? Tell him how much she was looking forward to the next time they fucked?

He slept after, always. They finished, and he would roll off of her and slip into immediate unconsciousness as if he had been hit over the head. He had begun mentioning that if she left while he was sleeping there was no way for him to tell if she had gotten up and left of her own free will or if she had been abducted. It was silly, even *he* had to know that, but he did have a point, which is why she began leaving the notes in the first place.

She never slept at his place, not even accidentally, not even after she had climaxed so long, so hard and so many times that she thought her legs wouldn't last long enough to carry her to her car. Her eyes remained pried open. She would never let herself get that relaxed, ever.

After finishing the note, she dressed in the dark, fastening her bra, pulling on a fresh pair of panties and stuffing the old ones in her purse.

She pulled her wrap dress over her head and straightened it over her hips and thighs. She stepped into her stiletto Mary Janes, gave the dimly lit bedroom a once-over, then reached for her keys.

She always made sure she left with everything she had come with, no panties left tangled in the sheets, no earrings on the nightstand. Those were games people played when they were trying too hard, forcing something. It was what people did when they didn't know their place.

She knew her place, and he knew his.

She glanced at the clock—11:45. At seven, the sun would peek through the blinds and stir him awake. He would roll over and remember she had been there but was gone. Not that he would expect her to still be there. Not that he had a reason.

He would read her note, call and see that she had gotten home okay and that would be that, the end of it, until one of them became restless and they found themselves together here again.

There was no in-between, no need for contact outside of this because that wasn't what they were. They weren't flowers and candy. They weren't candlelit dinners and family picnics.

They were this, this thing they shared in the late of night. They were notes on nightstands, brief phone calls and flirty text messages. That was all.

She thought of kissing him before she left, leaving a light peck on his cheek as he lay with his face pressed into the pillow. But that might wake him, and he looked so peaceful. It would be cruel to disturb him.

Besides, kissing could be a tricky thing. She knew that.

For the most part, they kept their lips to themselves. The occasional kiss on the neck or tummy was fine, his mouth sucking on her breasts—she rather liked that—but his lips on hers, her tongue curling its way around his, that was dangerous.

She knew this because he had kissed her once before, *really* kissed her.

They had been in front of her house and he had caught her off guard. He had almost missed, as a matter of fact, his warm soft lips landing on one corner of her mouth so that she had to readjust for comfort.

If nothing else about that night, she remembered how she felt when he held her by the elbows and pressed his lips to hers, how his tongue easing into her mouth made her feel weak and light-headed, and how, if he had let her go a second sooner, she would have fallen into a helpless heap at his feet.

She decided that very night it wouldn't happen again, and she assumed that eventually he had silently agreed it was too intimate. Kissing was something you did when you were in love, or hoping to get there.

And love complicated things, made what should be easy hard. They both knew that, had both been there and done that. They didn't speak of the past too much, but they had both been casualties, victims of its wrath. The ink hadn't yet dried on her divorce papers and he still kept his ex-girlfriend's toothbrush in his bathroom drawer.

But this time, with this thing, they had gotten smart, both grown clever enough not to make the same mistakes twice. That's why they got along so well. They understood that boundaries were important if you were to protect yourself. That was why it was easy for them to be apart and easy for them to be together. There were no expectations, no promises, no agreements.

There were no strings.

The music still played softly, something slow and sexy by Prince. He would sleep with it on repeat all night. She'd hear it in the background in the morning when he called.

She'd given him that CD, as a matter of fact. It was for his birthday because she hadn't wanted to just ignore the importance of the date, but she didn't want to make a big fuss over it either.

She wasn't his girlfriend, after all.

Of course, she thought about not giving him anything, thought he might read too much into even the smallest gift, but she wrapped up the CD anyway, pulled it from her purse as soon as she walked into his bedroom that evening and slid the glossy wrapped square across the bed in his direction.

"This for me?" he had asked, picking it up and flipping it over in his hand.

And she had fumbled over her words. "Yeah, 'cause we always listen to the radio and you know, sometimes commercials come on so—"

"No," he said, opening the present. "It's cool. I get it. Thanks."

And he had smiled and slid the CD into his boom box and pressed PLAY.

"I like Prince," he had said.

And she had said "Good," even though she had known it already. Knew it from the way he bobbed his head every time one of the songs came on the radio.

She knew because she paid attention, and she paid attention because they were friends and friends knew what friends liked. It had nothing to do with love, nothing at all.

She reached down now and straightened up the wrinkled sheet that covered his sleeping body. For one final time, she marveled at his silhouette, at his muscular legs and small waist, his powerful chest and strong arms. The heavy mass between his legs still showed strong through the covers though more than an hour had passed since his cock had been solid.

He was short for a man and had pale skin. He was small, but strong. Strong enough to turn her this way and that when they were in bed, strong enough to evoke screaming orgasms from her every single time.

She hadn't expected that. In fact, she hadn't wanted fireworks. She'd *had* fireworks and what had they gotten her? And it was true she preferred the tall and dark men who had given her all those fireworks, but they had made a fool of her every time.

That was why she was careful with him, kept him at arm's length at all times, made use of what he was good for and kept it moving. And even if she did get a little silly now and then and let an embrace last a few seconds too long, laugh too hard at a joke, that was okay. She was human, after all. She wasn't made of stone.

The key to it all was control; to catch herself before she went too far, before the feelings stirred too deep; to not do little things like let him see her completely naked, let him see that her tummy was still a little full from the twins; to not let him know that she ate too fast and laughed too loud.

She jumped when she heard the sharp crack of thunder outside. She looked toward the window where the blinds were pulled open, then blinked at the bright flashes of light.

She had hoped to be gone by the time the storm started, to be in her own bed asleep when all the rain came down. It had been *his* idea to fuck that last time, to make use of the hard-on he had gotten from just catching a glimpse of her breasts when the sheet fell around her waist.

Just then, he stirred beneath the covers. He rolled onto his back, his eyes fluttering open. He stretched his arms above his head.

He lifted his head off the pillow and peered out the window. "Is it raining out?"

"I think so, yes."

She had heard the first drop and knew that eventually the soft splatter would transition to a pounding force on the roof of his condo. She reached for the doorknob.

Then came the thunder again and the roar made her drop her hand. Her keys slipped from her fingers and fell to the floor.

He sat up in bed and rubbed his eyes.

"You don't have to go, you know," he said. "I would never send you out in weather like this."

She exhaled. "I'm a big girl. I can drive twenty minutes in the rain."

"I know you can," he said. "But I wouldn't want you to. I *don't* want you to." He rubbed the empty space next to him. "You can just lie down awhile, take a little nap with me 'til the storm passes over."

And at that moment, she couldn't think of any protest that would make sense, so she relaxed her shoulders, dropped her purse, and sat down on the bed. After all, would it be so bad if she stayed, if she lay beside him just a little while longer until the storm was all over?

She kicked off her shoes, kept her dress on and stretched out next to him.

She would lie here with him, but she wouldn't close her eyes. And if she closed her eyes, it would only be for a second, to let them rest a bit. She wouldn't relax. She wouldn't get comfortable. She *knew* what happened when you got comfortable, even a little.

Her spot was still warm. She settled into the dip in the mattress where she had rested just moments before. She scooted back, nestling into the empty space where his body curved.

He held her close, his arm draped across her waist, pressing her back into his belly. He rested his chin into her shoulder. She would allow this, for a while, just until things settled enough outside for her to escape to safety.

The lightning popped so loud it made her shake. He held her tighter and kissed her on the neck.

"You scared?" He spoke the words into her hair.

"No…yes. Always have been since I was a kid." She didn't see the need to lie.

"I never liked storms either," he said, but she figured he just wanted to make her feel better.

It did make her feel more comfortable, made the words come more easily.

"I remember I would run to my parents' room every time one started in the middle of the night. I'd bust through the door and jump in the middle of their bed and stay there until it passed." She stifled a giggle.

His breath was warm on her neck. "I bet you were cute when you were a kid."

She chuckled softly and thought about telling him about all the baby pictures her mom insisted on keeping all over the walls even though she thought they were the ugliest things she had ever seen. But she reached back and stroked his dick instead.

He seemed to welcome the distraction and she welcomed his hand sliding down her thigh and slipping beneath her dress.

He pulled her panties down. His fingers grazed her pussy. He began to rub slowly, softly. His thumb found her clit and pressed gently.

A groan escaped her lips and her hips began to grind against his crotch. She felt him rise behind her, thumping against the stretchy fabric that covered her ass.

He pulled the dress up and over her head and tossed the ball of fabric on the floor.

She was wet, so wet that his fingers slid easily and swiftly through the valley of her nether lips. She reached back and grabbed firm hold of his dick, coaxing him closer.

Finally, he pushed into her and her body relaxed. He held tightly to her hips, bringing her to him, pushing her away.

Her throat was suddenly dry, her mouth open, lips quivering.

They moved in rhythm with the storm, with the sound of Prince seeping softly through the speakers. They moved slow. They moved fast.

"I don't want to come yet." He whispered words into her ear that were a plea for mercy.

The thunder crashed outside his bedroom window and the rain came down hard. Cracks of lightning lit up the sky.

She pulled forward, releasing his dick, and rolled onto her back. She parted her legs and he climbed on top of her, sinking into her again. She wrapped her legs around his waist, limiting his depth, keeping him in the precise place that would cause the fluttering in her chest and the pull at the bottom of her belly. She burst into uncontrollable spasms, squeezing his cock between her legs.

She clasped her thighs tightly against his hips when she came. He breathed softly against her ear.

"You cheated," he said, laughing.

"Sorry." She smiled in the dark, dragging her fingernails lightly down his back.

She forced him onto his back then and straddled him, gliding slowly up and down his dick until he came.

After she caught her breath, she rolled over beside him.

She stared at the ceiling, looked around the room at things she had never noticed before. He had actual curtains in his bedroom and there were no piles of clothes in the corner of the room. He kept his space surprisingly neat, in fact.

She thought about scooping her dress off the floor and slipping it back on, to put at least that thin layer of fabric between them, but lying here with him like this felt strangely safe, oddly right, so she remained still, her moist skin pressed against his.

She didn't fight against him when he placed one strong arm around her and cradled her. She didn't protest when—like the rain outside—sleep came down and covered her like a sheet.

Her eyes fluttered open at just after three a.m. Her body was limp, her head heavy with sleep.

His voice was laced with grogginess. "Won't you stay? Tomorrow's Sunday and we don't have to do anything but relax. It'll be nice."

His grip on her wrist was firm. She looked back at him; his eyes were half-closed, his lips curved into a smile. He rubbed the back of her hand with his thumb, waiting for her answer.

She stood up and went about the business of dressing and gathering her things. She looked back at him when she was done, at the innocent hopefulness in his eyes.

And for a moment, just for a moment she considered it, allowed herself to imagine what it might be like to walk around his apartment barefoot, to fix him breakfast and clean his dishes, to lean against his shoulder on the couch as he watched ESPN.

She thought of telling him yes, that the idea sounded quite nice. But she knew that if she stayed, if she spent·the rest of the night lying in his arms, if she woke up with him the next morning, it would change things, there would be no turning back. So instead she leaned down, held her face close to his, and kissed him.

He closed his eyes and his lips relaxed against hers. Her tongue tickled the roof of his mouth, brushed quickly across his teeth.

It was enough to silence him, to push the idea far, far away, if only for the moment.

The moment passed quickly, so quickly in fact that she couldn't be sure he was awake, or even if she was.

Maybe she had dreamed it all, because just like that he was asleep again and snoring softly, lying there like always, unaware that she was even in the room.

She picked up the pen and pulled out a fresh piece of paper. She thought of what she should say now. It was always something cute and witty, something he could wake up to and smile at and toss aside without much thought.

Yet, somehow what she wanted to say now didn't sound cute *or* witty.

What she wanted to say weighed heavy on her chest. The words rose up like floodwaters, spilling into her throat, pouring into her mouth. She wrote them slowly, carefully, imagining the look on his face as he read them, wondering if he would smile, if his mouth would fall open in shock.

The words were strings pushing her forward and pulling her back. But as the minutes passed and her sanity found its way back, she pushed them down again, forced them to settle in her chest.

She scratched through the letters and ripped the paper to shreds. She balled it up and threw it in the trash. It would have been foolish to say the words, worse to write them. It was safer for them both if she didn't.

Outside was so quiet now, it was hard to tell there had even been a storm except for the droplets of rain that ran down the window.

She gathered the rest of her belongings in a hurry, rushing, because if she rushed, she could be out the door. If she hurried, she could be inside her car and halfway home before the sun peeked over the horizon, and awakened the city.

RADCLYFFE

ALL ABOUT US

ALTHOUGH I HAD A TRAILER ALL MY OWN, with words I was secretly very proud of printed on the side—RAFE BEVALAQUA, GENERAL CONTRACTOR—I still liked to eat lunch with the crew. Even on a sweltering July day in the middle of a half-finished subdivision where there wasn't a single tree to offer shade. Even when I had a little air conditioner in my unit where I could have taken a break in comfort. I liked eating with the guys, and that included the girls, because even though I was the boss, I needed them as much as they needed me. Besides, it wasn't all that long ago that I was one of them, a union carpenter with big dreams. Now I had my own company, which was a good thing, because I also had a wife and two kids.

Being a parent and the major breadwinner changes how you look at everything. Most of my day—hell, most of my *life*—was spent working so I could be sure they had what they needed. Not that Donna didn't work just as hard with a two- and four-year-old at home and a part-time job proofreading for a lesbian publishing company. But where my biggest worry used to be what restaurant I'd take Donna to for a romantic evening, now I worried about college funds and health insurance. That's the other thing that had changed. Since the kids, there wasn't a whole lot of time for us.

We were both dog-tired at the end of the day, and we didn't have the money or energy to do a lot of things we used to do when we first got together. We didn't go out clubbing or even out to dinner much anymore. Once in a while we caught a movie when my sister or Donna's mother could babysit, but we didn't party with our friends until all hours and we didn't stay up until dawn fucking like we used to. We were lucky if we could steal a couple of minutes on Sunday afternoon for few quick kisses and a fast come with a vibrator.

I missed coming home at the end of the day and finding Donna stretched out on a lounge chair in the backyard with a drink in her hand and a smile that said *I've been waiting all afternoon for you to take care of me*, when I'd go down on my knees right there and pull her skimpy panties aside and she'd already be wet and I'd lick her until she came with her fingers twisted in my hair and her pussy riding my face. I missed waking up on Saturday morning to her jerking me off nice and slow and easy while I just lay there, letting her do me like only she knows how. I missed strapping on a big dick and sliding inside her with long deep strokes, watching her face turn all dreamy and her eyes fill with tears because it felt so good and she was going to come so hard for me.

I loved my wife and I loved my kids. I loved my life. But sometimes I missed us like we used to be.

"Hey Rafe," Joe the electrician called. "You gonna eat what's in that lunch box? 'Cause if you're just gonna stand there with it, I'm good for seconds."

I stared at the black aluminum lunch pail in my right hand and realized I'd been standing outside my trailer daydreaming and blowing a good part of my lunch hour. Plus, I'd worked myself up pretty good just thinking about sex with Donna. My clit ached and my boxers were wet. "Yeah, yeah. Forget it, you mooch."

I pulled myself up onto a half-finished concrete wall next to Joe and a couple of other guys, ignoring the way my clit jumped as it was squashed against the seam of my khaki work pants. I flipped the top on the big box and pulled out my thermos, listening to the guys complain about the weather and the Yankees and the high cost of gas. When I reached in for my sandwich my fingers closed round something that definitely didn't feel like lunch, and I yanked my hand out so fast I almost dropped everything onto the hard-packed dirt at my feet. Fortunately, none of the guys noticed my reaction. Turning so no one could see what was inside, I opened my lunch pail again. The first thing I saw was the note in Donna's handwriting.

Rafaela. I'll be there at one. And I'll be hungry.

Underneath the note, neatly arranged next to the sandwich that Donna fixed for me every morning, rested my harness and a fat cock.

"What time is it?" I croaked.

"Five to one," Joe said. "Why? You got a plane to catch?"

I slammed the lid and jumped down. "I forgot. I got a...phone conference. I'll be busy for a while."

Then I ran for the trailer.

Once inside, I twisted the knob on the window air conditioner to high and hopped around the room on one leg and then the other trying to get my boots off. I finally took a breath, sat down on the small sofa pushed against one wall, unlaced my boots, and shucked my pants and underwear, all the time keeping one eye on my watch. Two minutes to go. I got myself geared up, redressed, and zipped just as a knock sounded on the metal door. The sound went straight to my clit, which was already pounding against the underside of my dick.

I opened the door and grinned at my wife. She was wearing very skimpy baby-blue shorts that matched her eyes and a halter top that tied behind her neck. Her blonde hair was loose and just touched her tanned shoulders.

"Hey, baby," I said, feeling as nervous as I would on a first date.

Donna stared at my crotch for a beat or two and then climbed the metal steps and brushed past me, bumping her pelvis into the bulge between my legs as she went by. "Hi, honey."

Knees shaking, I closed and locked the door. I leaned against it to regather my cool. "So where are the kids?"

"At my mother's." Donna dropped a shopping bag next to my desk and looked out the little window that didn't have an air conditioner in it. "Good. No one can see in."

"I got your note." My hands were sweating I wanted to touch her so bad, but this was her show. She knew what she wanted and whatever it was, I was going to give it to her.

"I noticed." She slid her hand between my legs and cupped the cock in my pants, jacking it slowly while she kissed me. Her tongue filled my mouth, thrusting slowly in and out to the rhythm of her hand working me. I untied her skimpy top, let it fall, and stroked the soft surface of her breasts with my fingertips. When I skimmed her nipples, already puckered and hard, she moaned and jacked me faster.

"You don't want to do that so hard, baby," I warned breathlessly. "Not unless you want me to come in my pants right now."

She eased up on me a little and ran her tongue around the rim of my ear. Her breath was hot and her voice husky. "Play with my nipples. That makes me so wet."

I knew exactly what it did to her. I could make her come if I tugged and twisted them hard enough and fast enough and long enough, but I knew that's not what she wanted. So I took her up to the edge a couple of times while she whimpered and clutched my shoulders and rubbed her pussy over the lump in my khakis. I backed off just before she was ready to shoot over the top and palmed her ass so I could buck my hips and bang her clit with the dick in my pants. She sagged against me.

"How you doing?" I asked, watching her struggle to focus on my face.

"I want to come," she whispered.

"Is your clit all swollen, baby?"

She sucked on my neck and rubbed herself all over the front of me. "You know it is."

"Do you want to come on my cock? Is that what you're doing here?" I walked her toward the little couch, my cock jammed into her pussy, while she nodded and made incoherent sounds. Then I sat down, spread my arms along the back of the couch, and opened my legs so the cock formed a tent in my khakis. "Show me."

Instantly, she was on her knees, fumbling with my fly. I bit back a groan when she pushed her hand inside my pants. She was so anxious to get at my rod she almost got me off from the pressure on my clit when she twisted the cock around to set it free.

"Jesus, take it easy, baby," I gasped. Any chance I had at being cool was gone.

She laughed and went down on my cock. She's a genius at timing the pumping action of her fist with the slow glide of her mouth down the shaft, so I can watch her suck me off and feel it in my clit just like it was a cock. The first time she did it to me I was going seventy on the interstate and she pulled my dick out and leaned over and blew me in about two minutes. I wasn't going to last two minutes now. I cupped the back of her head to slow her down.

"Not so fast. I want to come inside you."

"Do you? Sure about that?" She smiled up at me while she kept jacking and licking the head of my cock. Her eyes said she knew just how bad I wanted to come in her face. She kept at it until my legs went stiff and my belly got hard and I was one stroke away from going off. And then she stopped.

I groaned but I kept my hands clenched on the back of the couch, staring in a daze as she stood and slid her hand into her shorts. Her fingers twitched between her legs.

"I'm so wet."

She pushed her hand deeper.

"Mmm. Feels so good."

Her fingers danced faster and she threw her head back, eyes closed. I knew what she looked like when she came and she was almost there. I leaned forward and yanked her shorts down. Then I swatted her hand away.

"Get down here and fuck yourself on my cock."

She kicked off her shorts, straddled me on the couch, and sank onto my cock in one movement. Her head snapped back and she gave a high thin cry. She pushed up, almost all the way off, and sank down again to the hilt. She rode it that way, slow and deep, while I pulled on her nipples. I could see her clit each time she slid up the shaft. It was deep red, glistening, standing up between her parted lips.

"Feel good, baby?"

"The best," she gasped.

"Gonna come all over me soon?"

She nodded wordlessly, her body trembling. I knew what she needed, but I waited for her to ask. She managed another couple of strokes before she wrapped her fingers tight around my forearms and gasped, "Rub my clit."

I knew just how she liked it too. Back when we had all the time in the world, I used to watch her masturbate so I'd know just where to tease her clit to make her come. Now I pressed my thumb into the base of her clit until the head was bare and standing up, then I circled it with my fingers, dipping low to carry her cream up and over the top. She got superhard almost at once and I knew nothing was going to stop her now. Her nails dug into my arms and her hips flailed away at the cock while she half whispered, half cried, "I'm coming I'm coming I'm coming coming coming…"

I caught her when she fell into my arms, her legs still splayed on either side of my thighs, my cock still deep inside her. She always comes more than once when we do it this way, and while she circled her pelvis working up to another come, I could finally let go. I was almost sick, I needed to get off so bad. I slid the fingers I'd used to work her clit lower between our bodies, beneath the leather harness and onto the hot stone that was lodged between my thighs. I got the slippery shaft between my fingers and squeezed.

"Oh yeah. Oh baby, yeah."

Through half-closed lids I saw Donna raise her head to watch my face. "Are you going to come inside me now?"

I nodded, jerking my clit as best I could while she kept riding my cock. I couldn't breathe enough to talk.

"Ooo, I'm going to come again," Donna gasped, looking surprised. She pushed up so she was nearly sitting, her hands braced on my shoulders. I shoved my hand lower and pounded my clit while she pounded herself off on my cock.

I felt it coming from a long way off, that jangling of nerves that spreads from my clit straight into my pelvis and deep down the inside of my thighs. I waited until the last second, timing my come to hers, and then I let go of my clit and grabbed her hips and jammed her cunt down on my cock.

She was already crooning her come song when I yelled, "Here I come right inside you, baby."

I shot for so long, my hips jerking so crazily, that Donna got one more tiny come out of it before she pushed herself off and collapsed next to me on the couch.

"Oh my God, I haven't come like that in so long," Donna said.

I stared at my crotch where the dick bobbed in time to my pulsing cunt. My pants were soaked with come. My arms and legs felt boneless.

"I'm wasted and I can't go back to work looking like this."

"Aww, we really made a mess, didn't we?" Donna said, sounding not the least bit concerned. She kissed my neck, then took a tiny nip. I didn't even have the strength to move away. "I brought you clean pants, sweetheart."

I turned my head in her direction, my vision still hazy. "Yeah? You think of everything."

She fisted my cock and gave it a little shake. "Guess so."

I grabbed her hand, too sensitive for any more stimulation. "I'm done, baby. I can't get it up again. I'm sorry."

She sucked on my lower lip until I groaned, then kissed the sore spot. "You were very patient. Did you come nice?"

"Gangbusters."

"You held out a long time so I could come again." She kissed me, gently this time. "Thank you."

"Hey, you made it happen," I whispered. "So I wanted it to be great for you. I wanted it to be all about you."

Donna shook her head. "Every once in a while, honey, we need it to be all about us."

Like always, she was right. Which is exactly why I married her.

BROOKE STERN

AN UNEXPECTED LOVE STORY

A LOVE STORY SHOULD BEGIN WITH A CRIME, but when they busted me for shoplifting cheese from an uppity gourmet shop, I only expected a little bit of trouble—a fine or something—not love. How could I have foreseen someone like Tom?

In spite of an on-again, off-again case of kleptomania, I had never been arrested before. But on that night, my arrogance got the best of me and the way I slipped the cheese under my sweatshirt was just lazy. After a long evening and all the indignities of the legal system, I finally reconciled myself to calling the 1-800-GET-BAIL guy, read the numbers of my one credit card that wasn't maxed out, and walked out of the police station, hungry, tired and only slightly more hopeless than I had been the day before. I went to a grocery store and stole breakfast. I had cereal and milk at home, but at least walking out into the dawn with their most expensive prosciutto in my jeans made me feel more alive.

Then I went to a bookstore and stole a bunch of books on representing yourself in court. To make a long story short, I spent the time before my court date studying the law, falling another month behind on my rent, and maxing out my last credit card on an outfit for court. The judge, unfortunately, wasn't interested in my newfound enthusiasm for litigation and slapped me with a fine that I couldn't pay. Unsatisfied by my day in court, I decided it was a good time to file for bankruptcy. I studied even harder for the court date, this time at the law school library (it turns out legal books are hard to steal). I thought all of this would help, but the judge treated me like the other bottom-feeders in the courtroom. I was sitting on a bench in the hall crying when I met Tom and that's when the trouble really started.

He was next up to be called into court for a case he was prosecuting, and he sat down next to me on the bench to wait. The tissues I was using to dry my tears and blow my nose were piling up at my side. I first noticed him because he had grabbed the wastepaper basket from his side of the bench and held it in front of the bench where my used tissues lay. He waited patiently for me to see him, realize what he was doing, and brush the tissues off the bench and into the waiting receptacle.

"When's the execution?" he asked.

It took me a minute to get that he was joking.

"It's not that," I said, sniffling and straightening my hair. I tried to laugh, but it came out as a half cry, half sniffle.

"I know. I was watching you. You're not bad, but the mock trials in the first year of law school aren't going to help you defend yourself in bankruptcy court."

"I guess I should have seen it coming."

"A week after your shoplifting conviction? What were you thinking?"

"How did you know?"

"I work in the prosecutor's office. A friend of mine told me about the cute law school dropout who nearly got away with it."

"I nearly got away with it?"

"Yeah, he said you were great. But don't let it slip that I told you. It's our policy not to encourage criminals."

Impulsively, I hugged him, and I felt him go a little stiff as I pulled him into my sloppy embrace. "That's the nicest thing anyone's said to me since…well, I don't know when."

"How about you give me another chance to say nice things to you over dinner tonight?"

I knew, according to the latest slew of dating guides, that I wasn't supposed to accept last-minute requests, but who was I trying to fool? He already knew I was a broke kleptomaniac; I didn't have to hide that there weren't men lining up at my door.

"Sure."

"Stay here. I'll be done in an hour."

I grew fidgety and wanted to get up, go steal a coffee or at least go to the bathroom to fix my makeup, but something about the way he said "stay here" made me sit tight. Exactly an hour later, he emerged.

"Did you drive?"

"No." (I didn't tell him that I didn't even have a car.)

"I'll drive. Is Italian okay?"

"You mean a Ferrari or a Maserati?"

"No, I mean spaghetti or linguini."

"Oh. Okay."

The date was amazing. Sometimes a man can take you away from everything; he can make you forget your nerves, your insecurities, your worries and your failures. Tom made me feel beautiful and smart. For the first time in a long time, I felt loveable. For a while, it even seemed as if *he* was the insecure one. He warned me that he was the weirdo, the one who was hopelessly controlling and needed everything just so. While I suppose I should have been able to foresee the downside of all this, I found his honesty totally charming. Not only was he funny about his quirks, mocking his own craziness, but the order of his world also offered a welcome contrast to the chaos of my own life.

Finally, he looked me in the eye, reached across the table to clasp my hand and asked if I thought I might be able to accept him the way he was. He tried to make it a joke, but I could tell it really wasn't.

"Of course, Tom. Like I'm one to judge."

"Thank you, Nicole. It's such a relief to hear you say that."

"Can you accept me the way I am, Tom?" I asked, more out of a sense of parallelism than anything else. I figured it would be nice to be reassured, especially after I had gotten myself into so much trouble.

"Not a chance."

"What?"

"I warned you that I was rigid and needed things a certain way."

"But I can accept that."

"Good. Then I need you to stop stealing and get out of debt."

"But what if I need you to accept me the way I am?"

"Nicole, sweetheart, you don't even accept yourself the way you are."

Touché.

"And you propose to fix me?"

"Come back to my place and I'll tell you what I propose."

I could have been offended, or gotten scared, or mistrusted his motives, but instead I just let him pay the check, got in the passenger seat of his car, and went agreeably to his house. Tom made me very obedient.

His place was even neater than I had imagined it; totally modernist, black and white, and minimal. I expected the glass of wine and the awkward sitting next to each other on the couch and the fumbling first kiss, but instead we had hardly gotten in the door when Tom turned to me, looked me in the eye, and gave me the first of many thousands of direct orders.

"Take a shower. There's a clean robe hanging on a hook on the door that you can put on afterward."

I looked at him. Was he serious? Did he think I was dirty? Was this his way of bypassing the fumbling scene on the couch? Was he taking me for granted?

"Nicole, I'll never tell you to do something if I think you might regret it. You can always do whatever you want, but I think we'll be happiest if you do what I say."

He sounded both kind and menacing. I liked kind, but menacing felt electric. I turned and headed toward the shower, swaying my hips to whet his appetite.

The rest of the night went better than I dared expect. I got pretty hot with anticipation while I was in the shower. I emerged, still wet, in his robe and we began kissing. I wasn't even dry when he made me come for the first time, licking my clit right through my first orgasm and clear to my third. I had to pull him by the hair to make him stop and kiss me.

I ended up straddling him that first time. The second time he lasted longer and really had to fuck me hard to come at all. I don't come from fucking very often, but he gave me plenty of time to come twice more. He was behind me and I touched myself while he was doing it. Afterward, we cuddled until our sweaty bodies got chilly, and then we pulled up the covers and went to sleep. I've always thought that if you pay attention to how he fucks, you can tell whether a guy likes you or just likes fucking.

Tom liked me. I had no doubt.

The alarm went off frighteningly early the next morning. By the time I had stumbled into the bathroom and put on his robe, he had set a place for me at his table and made me an omelet. It was the first time I'd had anything but Pop-Tarts or cereal for breakfast since I stole that prosciutto.

"What are you going to do today, Nicole?"

It was an innocent enough question, but I don't think he meant it that way. He knew that bankrupt shoplifters don't usually make the right choices. It was his way of cutting to the chase. I was too scared to go where I knew he was going to take it, though, so I lied.

"I've got a job interview coming up. I'm going to go home and prepare."

I tried to be vague and ambitious, in hopes it would discourage further inquiry.

"Nicole, I'm a prosecutor. I spend my whole life taking apart people's lies. But I don't start work for another two hours. Just tell me the truth. What are you going to do today?"

"I don't know."

"That's better."

"I need to figure out what I'm going to do about repaying my debt."

"You should get a job."

"Duh."

"No, I mean you should get a job today."

"It's not that easy, Tom."

"I'm pretty sure that it is that easy, Nicole."

"Come on, Tom. I was thinking I really should go back to law school. Anyway, I haven't even updated my resume in eight months. Plus, I need to get resume paper and envelopes before I can even send any off."

"You mean steal resume paper and envelopes?"

It sounds like he was being mean, but he wasn't. He said it with a bit of a smile because he knew he was right, and I didn't deny it.

"Get a job by the end of the day and I'll buy you dinner and make you come twice as many times as I did last night."

"And if I don't get a job today?"

"Then I'll spank you and send you home without dinner or sex."

"But…"

"But what, Nicole? You didn't expect me to be so true to my word? Or is it the spanking thing?"

"It's… Well, it's both. It's everything."

"So, you know what you have to do, then?"

"Yeah."

How did he do that to me?

Then the most amazing thing happened: I got a job. Actually, I got three jobs and was scheduled to begin the following day at whichever of the three I decided to show up for. All three sucked, but at least I would end the day in less debt than I began it. I had imagined that I would be ashamed to grovel for work that was so below me, but I created a persona for each job who was better suited for groveling than I was. Besides, Tom's spanking remark gave me something else to think about.

The truth was, I kind of obsessed about it. I had always assumed that fetish was all kind of a joke, like French maid outfits or S/M dungeons. Something about it turned me on, but the fact that Tom had mentioned the concept worried me, too. How far was he willing to take things? I wouldn't find out that night, because his doorman buzzed me in at 6:55 with three job offers in my purse, in case he required proof. Dinner and many orgasms arrived as promised and I went to work at two of the three jobs the next day.

All went smoothly for a few weeks and I wondered if I might avert a spanking altogether until I lost both jobs in a single day. At that point, I realized I was certainly in for it. He hadn't named any specific punishment for getting fired twice in a day, but I was pretty sure it would be bad. Worse still, having been late, bitchy, petulant, and attitudinal with everyone else that day, I found that I couldn't turn off my attitude. I couldn't stop being bad, arriving late back at Tom's even though I could have arrived on time and adding a few additional misdemeanors to my accumulation of transgressions.

I was under the mistaken impression that these additional fuck-ups wouldn't really make a difference. I was going to get a spanking. What use was there in trying? Was I ever wrong.

It began with the looks of disappointment and him preparing to punish me while I waited, panties unceremoniously lowered around my ankles and hands behind my back holding my skirt up. Then, after hearing what he had in store for me but without any frame of reference to know what it would be like, I had to go into the bedroom and wait in the corner. Even alone, I was utterly humiliated. Who the hell was he to make me do this? I thought about leaving, but I knew I wouldn't. Something needed to put a stop to behavior that even I knew was ridiculous. If *this* could put a stop to it, it would be worth it, no matter how much it hurt.

I had always been bad with pain. As a child, I had begged off of even the most mild ordeals. Being special came naturally to me, but lying ass-up on Tom's lap didn't make me feel very special at all. I wondered how many asses had been there before mine. The spanks hurt like hell—was it any wonder that my thoughts were getting bleaker? My ego was getting as bruised as my butt. He was just doing his job—prosecuting the accused, holding the guilty accountable, and administering clear, immediate feedback. He was a prosecutor, through and through, and I knew how prosecutors felt about people like me. He was just getting his perverted kicks.

Tom was all about swift and clear reinforcement, of the painfully memorable kind. He was doing a good job, too. It was quite horrible. I had forgotten the way that one part of your body could be so possessed by agony that everything else disappeared. Spank. Spank.

Spank. The blows just kept coming, delivered mercilessly; each worse than the last. I imagined his point of view. He saw nothing of the agony, of the way my face contorted, the way my breath stopped, the way I felt like I would explode with pain and fear. All he saw was my fleshy ass bouncing and reddening as he brought his hand down on it over and over again. It was so unfair that it made me cry.

From that day on, I would always be on my best behavior after a spanking offense, knowing it was essential not to make things worse. Every little bit of behavior, whether good or bad, made a difference come spanking time. But I wished I hadn't had to learn that lesson the hard way.

"You don't understand how much it hurts, Tom!" I finally cried. "You don't understand. It's not fair."

"None of it's really fair, is it? Most shoplifters get away with it. Lots of girls have daddies who pay off their credit cards. None of it's your fault, is it?"

"Why do you have to hit me so hard? It's only making it worse."

"If you still think so afterward, then I'll never spank you again. But you'll thank me for it, Nicole. You really will."

"No, I won't. Never!"

I said it more in despair than denial. I would thank him for it because he cared. The more it hurt, the more I knew he cared. As if to emphasize the point, the spanking got harder until I couldn't talk or think or even cry. I saved up all the tears for after it was over, when they finally poured out because I hadn't gotten away with it. God, why did life always have to be so hard for me? Then Tom held me, and suddenly I felt as if maybe the next year wouldn't be as hard as the last one.

That's not to say the next few months weren't hard on my backside. I hated the spankings; loathed them, feared them, and avoided them every way I could, including behaving myself. But spanking also began to turn me on.

Why?

Well, it was how he did it to me. It was the way his masculinity and strength held me in place, grounded me, hurt me and yet contained all the chaos of my life. Spanking was the keystone of my private submission and exposure to him. My life was an open book to him; he could open me whenever and wherever he wanted. The spankings were a mixed bag. They reflected both his kindness—the attention and patience and way he cared for me—and his cruelty, too, his obsessive-compulsive rigidity, his cold adherence to the prescribed punishment, the inflexibility of it. The rules were the structure for the relationship. No rules, no relationship, and that, I confess, turned me on, too. I was an object. I liked being an object. It turned me on, whether I was his object to fuck, his object of desire, or the object of his rules, subject to his rule.

I knew our strange love wasn't for everybody, but it suited us just fine.

"The law makes us free." He liked to quote Kant and it felt true. It was our catechism. When I had believed myself to be free, I had really been a slave to my bad habits. With Tom, subservient to his elaborate order, I was truly free.

THOMAS S. ROCHE

THE BLONDE IN 1812

A S SOON AS SPENCE CRUZ saw the blonde coming like an angel out of 1812, he stopped dead in his tracks. A natural instinct for subtlety told him he shouldn't stare, but he couldn't help himself. She was a knockout.

Not to say that she was classically beautiful, the way you'd expect from a model or actress. There was just something special about the shape of her face, the smolder of her eyes, the curve of her body under the well-tailored black suit. The hem of that suit was maybe just a tad shorter than propriety would have dictated, showing Spencer that the blonde had a pair of the most incredible legs he'd seen in a long time. She carried a black purse over her shoulder and an Elmore Leonard paperback in her left hand.

There was something intriguing about her, something that said she was too classy to touch the Earth, and definitely too classy for the

Harrison Arms, a third-rate business hotel that was anything but classy. Sure, it had history, but it'd needed remodeling since at least 1960. Whereas the blonde in 1812 wasn't in need of any remodeling at all, that was for damn sure.

The blonde gave him the cold look of a woman who's just been checked out, knows she's just been checked out, and isn't giving an inch.

Spence watched, enraptured, as she walked down the hall and disappeared around the corner to the elevator.

He felt like an idiot.

Spence couldn't believe his luck, or maybe his lack of it. This late on a Tuesday night, the hotel restaurant was totally empty. But the maitre d'— if you could really call someone a maitre d' when he looked so badly in need of a good night's sleep (or a couple of uppers, maybe)—seated him one booth over and facing her. *Her.* The blonde in 1812. And she was even more of a knockout in the flickering candlelight, even sexier with her little round reading glasses on as she studied the menu.

Spence ordered Glenfiddich, thinking it might offset the effect of the threadbare red carpet and sleazy booths.

Dawdling over whether to get a steak or a Caesar salad, Spence tried hard not to look at her, but failed. Engrossed in the menu, she gave no indication of noticing him—except for the faint upward flicker of her eyeballs when he was imprudently staring at her with dreamy eyes. Finally, Spence decided this was ridiculous.

Picking up his drink, he took the few steps over to the blonde's booth.

"Excuse me," he said, as politely as he could manage.

The blonde put down the menu, stared at him as if only slightly perturbed.

"I...ah, I noticed you were on the same floor as me—I figured since we're both dining alone...maybe you wouldn't mind some company? I'd even love to buy you dinner."

She stared for a few seconds, as if amazed at his gumption. But then she smiled.

"Especially since it's Valentine's Day, is that it?"

"No, no, nothing like that," he said. "And besides, it's not Valentine's Day."

"Yet," she said with a glance at her watch.

"Yet."

"All right," she said. "Why not? But mine's on my company, so don't bother."

"Mine, too," he said, and winked.

Her name was Julia—no last name. She lived in New York. He told her his name was Steve, from L.A.; two lies. She looked suspicious, and thereafter on the two or three occasions when she referred to him by name, it sounded like she was putting quotes around it.

"You know, there's a lot of history in this hotel," he told her.

"Is that right?" She toyed with the stem of her wineglass. Cabernet sauvignon, to go with the steak she'd ordered.

"In nineteen-sixty, Sam Giancana had Jacob Anzer killed in the barbershop. Same way Albert Anastasia got killed in New York—hot towels on his face and everything."

"I take it Sam Giancana is some kind of gangster."

"Was. Boss of all bosses, at least in Chicago."

"And…are you some kind of gangster?"

"I would hardly go spouting obscure tidbits of Chicago Mafia history if I was, would I?"

"Cop, then?"

"No, no."

"Lawyer."

"Keep guessing."

"Wannabe mystery writer."

"Bingo. How'd you guess? It's the white socks, isn't it?" He was wearing black silk socks and Dexters, or he never would have made the crack.

"No, that'd make you a cop. Well, if you're not here to kill anybody or bust gangsters, what is it you're in Chicago for? Oh, damn, sorry—I ended my sentence with a preposition there." Her voice dripped sarcasm, but she didn't crack a smile.

"You should never end your sentence with a proposition," he said, and regretted it the second he'd said it.

Julia laughed, as if vaguely amused by his forwardness. She toyed with her wineglass some more.

"Sorry, that was in bad taste," he said, reddening.

"Oh, so you're saying you *want* me to end my sentences in propositions."

"I sell computers for interstate trucking companies," he said quickly, smiling broadly to make it painfully obvious that he was changing the subject. "I was here closing a deal."

"They send you all the way to Chicago from L.A. in the middle of February for that?"

"Well, I would prefer it if they sent me in May, sure, but it's a half-a-million-dollar system. In this business, what the customer wants, the customer gets."

She whistled, her eyes sparkling. "You don't say."

"You?"

"Considerably less than a half a million dollars." She smiled.

"Uh…no, I mean what do you do for a living?"

"Oh, a little of this, a little of that…." She smirked. "I'm in advertising. I have a new client in Chicago."

"In town long?"

"I have a six a.m. flight."

"Tomorrow?"

"Tomorrow."

"Ouch."

"Well, I'll be glad to get home. I hate the Midwest this time of year." She got a crazy smile on her face. "Are you married?" she asked.

He wrestled with that one for a full five seconds. "Yes. I'm married. Happily, to a great woman."

"Well, well," Julia sighed. "She's lucky to have a husband who speaks so well of her. I wasn't making a pass at you, just curious."

"Well, thank God for that," he smiled, trying hard to pump up the mojo and not succeeding very well. "And you?"

"Sometimes," she said. "Sometimes not."

"That's convenient."

"I'm a woman of convenience. You have any kids?"

"Not yet," he said. "We're planning to try, but we haven't really started yet."

"Uh-huh. Casanova's trying to get his wife pregnant. Soon to be a father, but he has dinner with strange women while on business trips."

"Hey! I thought you said you weren't making a pass at me."

"I'm not," she said, her tongue teasing the rim of her wineglass. "Yet."

He laughed, awkwardly, expecting her to say something more, but she didn't. She just let him squirm.

"This is getting…interesting," said Spence.

Julia finished off her fourth glass of red wine.

"To answer your question—yes, I'm married," she said. "And very much in love."

"With your husband?"

She mocked offense. "Of course, you cad. Of course I'm in love with my husband."

"Which is why you aren't making a pass at me."

"Yet."

"Of which you keep reminding me."

"I'm very much in love with him, he's very much in love with me. That doesn't mean…well, I'm sure you know how it goes."

"No, actually, I don't really know how it goes. Want to tell me?" he said, staring at the way she ran her fingers through her lustrous blonde hair. "You have the most beautiful hair."

"Oh, let's not start that," she sighed.

"Yet?"

She giggled, an oddly girlish sound from a woman who smoldered as much as this one. "No promises."

"I'll save up my compliments, but it's tit for tat. If you're so much in love with your husband, why are you having dinner with me?"

"Because you came up and invited yourself, 'Steve.' "

When she saw his face reddening, she giggled again. The waiter cleared away the remains of steak and lobster, asked if they wanted coffee. Julia motioned for another glass of wine, a wicked look on her face.

"I'll have Valium and a joint," said Spence.

"Sir?" The waiter looked genuinely confused.

"Just a cup of coffee." He polished off his second Glenfiddich.

"You think that's wise?"

"What's that supposed to mean?"

"Hotel coffee can be deadly. It's ten o'clock."

"Oh, the coffee. I thought you meant the Valium. You're the one with the six o'clock flight."

"Oh, I sleep like a baby on long flights. I could stay up all night if I had to."

"Uh-huh."

"Still getting interesting?"

"More interesting every minute."

She gave him a suspicious sidelong look, and toyed with the rim of his tumbler. Spencer felt himself getting hard under the table.

"So you didn't answer my question. If you're so in love with your husband, why are you having dinner with me?"

"I *did* answer your question. If you're so in love with your wife, why are *you* having dinner with me—especially the night before Valentine's Day."

"Now, I didn't say I was in love with my wife."

"Oh, you bastard! So you don't love your wife, and you spend Valentine's Day with strange women in hotels."

"No, I *do* love my wife. But what I said was that we were very happy, and she's a wonderful woman. Besides, I'm hardly spending Valentine's Day with a strange woman in a hotel, am I?"

"You tell me," she said. "So let's put it another way. Why are you having dinner with a strange blonde and making eyes at her?" She giggled. "Oh, did I say that? Sorry, it must be the wine."

"Must be. I'm not making eyes at you." He regretted it the moment he said it, because they both knew that he *was* making eyes at her— for God's sake, it would have been awfully hard to miss.

"So, then, why?" Spence felt her leg brushing up against him— probably by accident. The waiter brought Julia's wine and Spence's decaf.

"Who's seducing whom here?" Spence said.

Her leg vanished. "Nobody's seducing anybody, Romeo. Answer the question." She sounded offended, but she was smiling a little.

Spence shrugged. "We have an agreement. Things happen. You're married; I'm sure you know that as much as I do. There's no point in pretending that they don't, and there's no point in letting them affect a lifetime commitment, right?"

"As long as you wear a biohazard suit."

"Well, this is the twenty-first century."

"So what you're saying is that cheating on your wife is okay as long as you go back to her."

"Jesus, it's not as coldhearted as that. It's not really cheating if you both agree to it, is it?"

"Ask Hillary Clinton. It's not really cheating if you both *do* it."

"Now *that's* coldhearted."

"Is it? Then I guess I'm coldhearted."

"And you did *not* answer my question. You said you were having dinner with me because I came up and invited myself, but that's bullshit. You could have told me to fuck off."

"Do you become progressively more foulmouthed as the evening wears on?"

"Sorry," he said.

"Oh, I was hoping you do."

"Give you something to look forward to?"

"Uh-huh." She sipped her wine.

"So why are you here?"

She laughed, almost bitterly.

"Because I figured it might be fun to fuck you."

It took a minute for that to sink in.

"You mean fuck with my mind?"

Julia rolled her eyes, and Spence felt her hand, warm and firm, finding its way into his lap, discovering his hard-on. An instant's embarrassment was replaced with a flood of excitement as he stared into her gorgeous eyes, as she smiled at him.

"Jesus Christ, 'Steve,' what do they teach you in the computer industry? I mean *fuck* you. You *do* do that sort of thing in Los Angeles, don't you?"

Her place was three doors closer to the elevator, so they went there. Looked like she'd left for dinner in a hurry: the bed was a tangle of expensive lace panties, bras, camisoles in navy blue, forest green, deep burgundy. She killed the light and swept her sweet nothings from the bed with a single graceful movement. She took an instant to take out her long gold earrings.

"The way I like to do things," she said in a soft, husky voice as she turned her head to look at him over her shoulder, "these would *definitely* get ripped out." She set the earrings on the nightstand, kicked off her shoes, then put her arms around him. The warmth of her body enticed him; as they came together, she could no doubt feel he was still hard—maybe harder than ever. She kissed him once, lightly, on the lips, and then grabbed him around the waist and pulled him hard onto the bed. He went down easy.

She smelled like cinnamon, just a hint of it under the faint smell of her clean silk suit. The first kiss felt electric; the taste and texture of her lips and tongue were like nothing Spence had ever felt. She kissed him hungrily, nipping at his lower lip like she was badly in need of a second meal. Meanwhile, her hands crawled slowly but insistently up his chest—not undressing him, just touching, feeling, exploring. He put his fingertips on her face and kissed her hard, thrilled at the way her jaw worked gently as she coaxed him with her tongue. He ran his fingers through her blonde hair and she shook her head just enough to scatter her mane fetchingly on the pillow as the light from the window scattered over them. Her hands found his shoulders, gripped them as if measuring, weighing him.

Spence kissed her hard again, harder, unbuttoning her blazer and slipping his hand inside to run it over the firm, small swells of her slight breasts under the thin silk camisole. Her nipples were hard—very hard—and he stroked them gently at first before pinching them experimentally, those two actions coaxing a low moan of increasing volume from her pretty lips. He kissed her again and slid his hand up into her camisole. The feel of her naked breasts against his fingertips sent a shiver through him; she arched her back as he pulled up the camisole and lowered his mouth to her neck, kissing his way gently down.

He was heading for her nipples—she knew it, both of them knew it—but he saw no particular reason to rush things, and he lingered over the delicate slope of her throat, the line of her collarbone, even her shoulders. Then his tongue trailed a path down toward her breasts, and he took one sensitive nipple into his mouth.

"Oh God," she said, squirming her way out of the blazer, the camisole. "Jesus, don't stop that." The tangle of camisole and blazer fell to the floor, and Spence's left hand roamed over the naked curves of Julia's upper body while his right cupped her breast, guiding it into his mouth rhythmically as Julia squirmed. She groped at his shirt, got it unbuttoned, pulled him down closer so she could feel his chest against her belly as he suckled on her breast. She could no doubt feel his erection pressing against her leg, and probably wished she could get his pants off without having him take his mouth off of her breast. But she couldn't, so she pushed him back slightly, saying, "Promise me you'll go back to that in a minute," and her hands found his belt. She unfastened it quickly, trying to get his pants right off, but her hand just sort of slipped naturally into them, like it was meant to be there, and as she curved her fingers around his hardness she guided him onto his back, and then her lips were around his thick head.

"Shouldn't you be using—" he began, but it dissolved into a moan as she swallowed him. "Holy shit, that's something else," he sighed.

"It's supposed to feel good," she said a few seconds later when she came up for air.

"Oh, it does," he said, and she went back to it. She was now lying partially opposite him, and his hand lightly trailed up her stocking-clad thighs, sliding up to her panties. He worked his fingers underneath, found her wet. She moaned softly as he penetrated her with one finger, then, using her whimpers as a guide, two. Her mouth never stopped bobbing up and down on him. God, it felt so illicit, so wicked to let a stranger do that to him. He hadn't done that since...well, for a long time. But God, it was divine. Maybe that's why he did what he did, so easily; he worked his hands under the waistband of her panties, started to slip them off—

Her lips lifted off of him, hovered perhaps half a millimeter away, and she panted, her breath warm on his spit-slick shaft. "Shouldn't your mouth be full?"

And then she was back down on him, and squirming out of her panties as he pulled up her skirt and lifted her onto him. She shifted her body, settling down on top of him with her bare breasts on his stomach, her mouth on him, her legs spread around his face, finding that their bodies fit together perfectly, that with her back arched just so, his mouth was in just the right position to...

Julia shuddered, moaning softly as she felt his tongue wriggling into her, teasing her entrance, then on her clit. A surge of pleasure went through her, and Spence tasted a fresh flood of her salty juice. His lips pressed to hers, he let his tongue work, every now and then suckling on her clit gently and then a little more firmly as her moans told him she liked it—she liked it a lot. While she writhed, spread, on top of him, he kicked off his Dexters and socks. She shifted her body so he could lift his ass off the bed, and she wrestled his pants off of him.

Under the slightly-too-short-for-propriety skirt, Julia was wearing tasteful stockings, businesswoman-beige. But they were clipped to a lacy, skimpy garter belt that framed her ass beautifully. Spence's hands caressed the contours of her buttocks as his tongue wriggled into her, worked her clit. Soon the thrusts of her mouth came more slowly, and then her head was lifting, her back arching as she squirmed herself down harder onto his face. She still had her hand around his shaft, but she wasn't sucking him any longer.

She was pumping her hips up and down, rubbing her cunt almost violently on his face, but he stuck with her, his tongue feeling the swell and throb of her clit as she moved against him. She whimpered at him not to stop, not to ever stop, and then she came, hard, the spasms of her sex insistent against his lips as he rode her clit hungrily, listening to her come. God, she made a lot of noise when she came—screaming, almost at the top of her lungs, wordless, descending into a faint stream of positive expletives and a labored sob as she finished coming.

Then, before he could even recover from the motion of her pumping thighs, she was on him again. One hand gently caressed his balls while her mouth worked. He knew he was getting close, and he didn't want to come yet—but Julia wasn't about to stop. Clearly, she wanted his orgasm and she wanted it now, and the pumping motion of her hand around his base told him that it was pointless to resist. The sense of being utterly under this stranger's control drove him over the edge, and he felt himself throbbing and spasming as he flooded her mouth— and he expected her to pull away, but she didn't.

The vague sense of guilt he felt at letting this stranger taste him was offset by the fact that she'd all but demanded it. When she'd swallowed it all, she licked his softening cock clean, slowly in tiny strokes. But she didn't stop, even then; she moved down to his balls, and gently licked those, giggling as she heard the surprised, slightly frightened moan from his lips.

"You like that?"

"I like that very much," he said softly. "But it's…intense."

"Mmmm, intense," she sighed. "Just the way I like it." And she started to lick his balls, more gently than before, while she cradled his soft shaft in her hand. When Spence craned his neck slightly, she got the picture and snuggled down on top of him, her legs spread just so, and his mouth found her again, bringing moans from her lips as he teased her further. "Gentle," she gasped at one point when he licked her a little too hard—"I'm always so sensitive after I come. But you guys know all about that, don't you?"

Spence kept licking, as gently as he could manage, and her moans rose slightly in pitch as he did. The whole time, she caressed his balls with her tongue and even rubbed his organ gently with her thumb, which brought a violent spasm from Spence's body the first four or five times, but when she asked if she should stop he said "No." And the fifth or sixth time, he didn't jerk. He started to harden.

"Mmmm," said Julia rapturously. "That was easier than I expected it to be." And her mouth descended on him again. But after a minute Julia lifted her body off of his and said, "I hope you don't think I'm some slut who gets off on having oral sex with strange men in hotel rooms."

"Um…well, I…" Spence stammered.

"Because that's hardly all I like," she smiled, sliding off of him and unfastening her garter belt.

He didn't even question it as their naked bodies slid together between the clean, starched hotel sheets. Didn't even think twice as she mounted him, took his hard cock and pressed the head naked against her entrance. Her face and breasts were flushed deep red. She looked more beautiful than she ever had.

He answered her with a moan, as she sank down onto him.

It was one of those experiences where every movement is magic, where the physical sensations mirror the sense of liberation, or maybe of union. Either way, they did it for forty-five minutes, first Julia bucking and pitching, erect on top of Spence while his hands caressed her breasts and then her face. Next he pulled her down onto him so his mouth could find her breasts, his tongue driving her to a second orgasm as she came down hard, thrust after thrust, on top of him and used her right hand to stroke her clit, harder than Spence would ever have dared. Then they rolled, smoothly and miraculously, so that he did not leave her body for an instant, and Julia wrapped her legs firmly around her lover's body as he brought her to a third orgasm and then came himself, harder than the first time, inside her.

Afterward, she asked him if he minded if she had a cigarette. He looked shocked.

"What? Are you asthmatic?"

"No, you just…you don't seem like the smoking type."

"Well, I'm not…except after incredibly hot sex with strange men in hotel rooms."

Which flattered Spence so much that he kissed her, hard, again, and Julia didn't get to have her cigarette until after Spence had caressed her all over and entered her twice from behind, and their bodies had nestled together like spoons while he came inside her for the second time.

"I never come more than twice," he said as he watched her full lips around the filter of the cigarette. "You're incredible."

Which is when she did it: proved she was even crazier than he'd thought she was. "Well if you sometimes come twice, then I'm hardly satisfied with only having made you come three times," Julia smiled, and her hand cupped his soft cock. Spence had *never* come four times in one night, but after a short rest she managed to do it with her hand and mouth, climbing on top and guiding him into her barely ten seconds before his fourth orgasm shuddered through his sweaty, exhausted body, just as Julia's alarm went off.

He fell asleep while she was in the shower. When he woke up, she was gone.

She'd left a note on lined pink notepaper, written in purple ink.

> *Danger is a drug*
> *Best savored with loved ones.*
> *Happy Valentine's Day, "Steve."*
> —*The Blonde in 1812*

To Spence's surprise, Julia had written an email address—Hotmail, of course, which he found oddly illicit and thrilling. He showered in her bathroom, where he could still smell her scent. Then he put on his dirty clothes and walked three doors down to his room, to get ready for his eleven o'clock flight to Phoenix—to sell a six-figure system to a company that shipped Popsicles.

Spence and "Julia" probably wouldn't have continued meeting, every Valentine's Day, at the Harrison Arms in Chicago, if it hadn't been for what happened six weeks later—oddly enough, on April Fool's.

But in the meantime, Spencer Cruz didn't feel the need to discuss what happened with his wife—except for one brief comment shortly after he returned home to their Berkeley house.

"Love the blonde hair," he told her, and she just smiled, knowingly, and didn't say anything. They screwed each other senseless that night.

He thought it was a joke at first, given that it was April Fool's Day, after all. He thought it was Mandy's idea of a practical joke to show him the little test strip with its oddly elliptical plus sign. But the rich blush of her face, and the broad smile she was trying, and failing utterly, to suppress, told him that it wasn't a joke.

"And that's not all," she whispered into his ear as if telling him a great, illicit secret. "I can't be one-hundred-percent sure, but I'm almost positive it happened that night…."

"You're kidding," he said.

She nodded, and kissed him, hard. He held her and smiled—just smiled, ear to ear.

Years later, when Harry Julian Cruz had to explain the derivation of his first name—"Harrison"—to casual acquaintances, he always claimed to be named after Harrison Ford and Julian Sands, which is what his parents had told him. The details would doubtless have been too weird for an adolescent to accept about his parents—but once he was old enough, he did start to wonder what possessed his folks to leave him at Grandma's and visit Chicago every year for a single night in the dead of winter, the night before Valentine's Day. He decided he'd probably figure it out when he was older.

JOLENE HUI

PARKER'S MUSTACHE

LOOFNESS WAS ONE OF MARK'S strongest qualities. But it hadn't always bothered me. We used to say that we'd always be hand in hand—walking along the beach, eating sushi, watching horror movies at night, and enjoying long sessions of lazy sex on weekend mornings. But somehow that all got out of hand when spring came. We were both thirty, and had been through our crazy twenties and five years of obsessive love with each other. Mark had become distant lately, often closing himself up in his study and not coming out for days. He was working intensely on his book, convinced he had to finish it in the next two weeks. I was lonely and longed for the days when we actually spent time together.

I missed his love.

When Mark's brother Parker showed up on our doorstep on a day in May, I wasn't sure exactly how to handle the situation. He had

Mark's dark cocoa complexion, but his hair was darker, his skin rough, and, unlike Mark, he had facial hair. His mustache and sideburns were rugged and long. I had never liked that sort of thing before, but on Parker, it was the sexiest thing I'd ever seen. My heart almost stopped when I opened the door and saw him standing there. I could barely utter "Can I help you?" as we locked eyes. His eyes were a glimmering and breathtaking blue. "I'm Helen," I said, and stuck my hand out to have it grabbed by Parker's large and strong one.

"Nice to meet you, Helen." He gently kissed the top of my hand, his mustache tickling my delicate knuckles.

I wandered around in a blur the rest of the day. As Mark and Parker reminisced about old times, I took it all in.

"Could you grow sideburns and a mustache like Parker's?" I asked Mark in bed that night, trying to speak quietly as Parker was in the next room.

"No," said Mark. "He always had better facial hair. Mine is horrible. That's why I shave every day."

Parker was just passing through on his way to visit some friends in Baja. He had made this stop in San Diego specifically to see his brother.

"What's the deal with you and Parker?"

"What do you mean?" Mark rolled away from me.

"Well, we've been together five years and I've hardly heard about him."

"I talk about him all the time."

"Yeah, I know, but I've never met him 'til now. I was beginning to wonder if he was just an imaginary figure."

"Nope. He's real and apparently still crazy—he kept talking about some jet he is going to buy."

"What's wrong with having dreams, Mark?"

And with those idealistic words, we both fell asleep. I dreamt of Parker's sideburns, mustache, and lips.

The next day was a Sunday. I walked downstairs in the morning to find Parker in the kitchen scrambling eggs.

I poured myself a cup of coffee from the pot he brewed. It smelled fabulous.

"This definitely isn't my coffee. What kind is it?" I yawned and held the mug under my nose.

"Just something from Hawaii I've had for a while." He scooped the eggs onto the plate and put cheese on them. I couldn't help but scoot closer to him. I seemed to be magnetically drawn to his side. He was freshly showered; his skin smelled clean.

His hands were massive, and looked like they'd worked hard, the joints slightly swollen and the skin reddened by weather. I pictured them reaching around my waist pushing me against the wall, his mouth on mine; sliding all over my body. I could almost feel his hard torso pressing against the hot skin under my flannel pajamas. The long stubble on his cheeks rubbed against my soft skin. I let his hands push down my pajama bottoms, the air hitting my pussy—making me gasp. His knuckles grazed my pubic hair. The taste of coffee was on his lips as they reached mine. When he inserted a finger into me I dug my teeth into his shoulder to keep from exclaiming.

The sound of footsteps jolted me from my fantasy.

It was Mark, his hair mussed and his robe tied nicely around his waist.

"Good morning, honey," I said, my coffee mug still in my hands, my pussy wet from my fantasy of having Parker's knuckle buried inside it.

"Hi." Mark poured himself a mug of coffee, took a bagel from the counter and walked straight into his office.

"He has to finish a project in the next couple of weeks," I explained to Parker. I looked down at the beautiful plates of eggs on the counter.

"I know. He told me," he said, grabbing a fork. "Why do you think I chose to visit this weekend? Did you think I really wanted to spend time with my brother?"

I smiled, watching his eyes crinkle up.

"Well, there's a lot to do here. You can enjoy the beach, relax, work out; we have a full setup out in the guesthouse."

When Mark got stressed out, he'd spend hours in the gym in the guesthouse to cool off.

"I think I might just go sit in the sand. Take it all in." He washed his plate, and promptly set about cleaning up the mess in the kitchen.

He was a fucking dream come true.

"If you want to go for a run, I'm going for one in an hour," I said as I rinsed my dish and put it in the sink. I could feel Parker hovering around me in our small kitchen. When I turned around he was right behind me. "Excuse me," I said, stumbling by him, feeling his breath on my cheek.

"I'll be ready for the run in time. I'll be outside waiting."

I watched him walk outside and wanted to go after him, lure him into the guesthouse and straddle him. Instead I went into my bedroom to change clothes.

Mark was still in his study when I finished my stretching. I'd hardly heard a word from him. He and I used to go for runs together all the time. I wasn't sure if I could live with this much longer. Isolation did not suit our relationship, but I was still too much in love with him. At night in bed I could feel the electricity between us and when he kissed me while placing his fingers softly on my cheek, I'd melt. The moistness of his tongue was perfect and the flavor of his skin was still my favorite. Yet, he wasn't interested in sex much anymore and, as a result, I was out of my head and unsatisfied. This phase would pass. I knew it would. These sexual hiatuses always passed after he completed stressful projects. Sometimes, though, I worried that his drive and focus on work wouldn't pass and that he would become so involved in it that memories of me would fade away completely and I'd sleep alone at night while he passed out at his desk in his robe.

When I went outside, I saw that Parker was shirtless, and his chiseled abs and dark skin sent my heart into rapid hummingbird mode.

On our run, we chatted briefly about our lives. Parker had been married and divorced twice and did not think he would ever marry again. He spent most of his life traveling. He had invested really well in his early twenties and had quite a lot of money to play with. He was a real estate broker who spent most of his time working out, being with his friends and enjoying fine wine. His smile wrinkles proved his happiness. I wanted in on his world, if only for a second—or maybe a half hour or so.

We stretched, the sweat shining on our bodies. Mark was still inside, buried in his work.

"Do you want to see the weight room?" I asked, my head between my stretched-out legs.

"Isn't it in the guesthouse?" Parker was doing a tricep stretch, the sweat pouring down his arms.

I stood up and nodded.

"Yeah, I'd like to try it out."

"So would I," I said, leading him to the door.

As soon as I clicked the door shut behind us, my hands were all over his body. I was hungry for him and wanted to feel his facial hair on my slick body. He quickly responded, pushing his tongue into my mouth and moaning. His hands went straight to my breasts and massaged them through the material of my damp sports bra. I ran my hands up and down his chest and licked his lips. His facial hair tickled my face; it was just long enough to be soft. His mouth was everywhere—licking, scratching, tickling, tasting. Soon, we were on the floor, the hard carpet bristling against us. Parker grabbed my sports bra and rolled the tight fabric up my body and over my head, freeing my breasts. Only briefly did it occur to me that Mark could walk through the door at any second and find his brother and wife sucking each other's body parts in a fury of passion. But the thought soon ended and by that time, we were both naked and entwined. I was on my back, ankles in the air, Parker's face buried in my pussy: his facial hair was rubbing against my inner thighs, his luscious tongue tasting every part of me.

"Oh Parker," I moaned, placing my feet on his shoulders. "Your face."

He continued to lick and suck my cunt, until I couldn't take it anymore and came. I bit my hand to keep from screaming. My thighs twitched with pleasure. When he kissed me, I almost came again—

I tasted myself all over his mustache. I pushed him onto his back and straddled his face. I wanted his mustache on me.

He didn't object, but merely put his thumbs on my inner thighs and continued to lick and suck. It felt as if my hips were meant to move on top of his face this way. A scream escaped my throat and Parker used his rough hands to lay me out on the floor. With his right hand over my mouth, he balanced on his left arm and shoved his hard cock inside me. His hand muffled my scream. He fucked me hard and quickly. I spread my legs farther apart so that he could move easily. Underneath his hand I moaned and panted. His hand held a mixture of our scents. I licked his palm as he finished inside me.

Later that afternoon, Mark decided to come out of his study to take a shower. Parker was outside talking on his phone and I was inside reading.

"Have you gotten anything done today?" I asked curiously, as Mark walked around with a towel on.

"A little. What have you done today?"

Visions of fucking Parker in the guesthouse filled my mind. I could feel myself getting wet thinking about it. "Parker and I went for a run. Then I stretched and showered."

"Hmmm." Mark toweled off his hair. "I think I want to grill some steaks tonight. Parker said he had some kind of marinade recipe he wanted to make for us."

"Are you going to spend any time with your brother?" I asked, even though I really hoped he would keep himself locked up, leaving Parker to me.

"You know I'm busy with this, honey," Mark said, leaving the living room where I lounged.

I pretended to be reading when Parker came inside. "Is Mark out of his cave?"

I thought my face might be getting hot. "Yeah, and he said you guys were going to grill tonight."

"Actually, I've invited my friend Shelby over for dinner, too. I hope you don't mind." A huge bullet of jealousy shot through me. Well, of course Parker had friends. Female ones.

"The more the merrier." I buried my face in my book.

We ate dinner on the backyard deck that night. Shelby was smoking a cigarette and talking about the meaning of life. She seemed to be the type of chick Parker might want to hook up with—short hair, little makeup, outdoorsy, tough, someone he could bang anywhere, who wouldn't get pissed off if her hair or makeup got messed up.

I sipped a glass of red wine and stared at the stars above our shed. The shed used to be a workshop, but hadn't been used as that in years. Instead we just shoved our storage in it and decorated the outside. There was a ladder leading up to the top for a secret getaway spot. If you were on the far side of the shed, no one in the backyard could see you. It was a special hiding place, surrounded by trees.

I'd been making eye contact with Parker all night, thinking about what had happened earlier. I wanted so much to reenact the scene at least once before he had to leave.

"I could use some vodka," said Shelby, stamping out her cigarette.

"Oh," I said, "I'm sorry. We don't usually have hard liquor on hand." We were more the wine-drinking type.

"I could go pick some up, if you want," Mark offered.

"It's not a big deal. I was just thinking that I wanted a little after-dinner drink." Shelby lit another cigarette.

"Why don't we take a drive and pick some up," Mark said. "I'm in the mood for some dessert, too."

Mark was helping me fulfill my fantasy and he didn't even know it. "That sounds like a good idea. Parker and I can stay here. I'd like to show him the view from the shed anyway."

Shelby said, "You know Parker, you should really shave. I love you clean shaven. I'm getting sick of this mountain-man look." She and Mark left.

Parker's hand was warm as I tugged on it and led him toward the shed.

"Helen…"

"No one can see us up here. Trust me."

I led him up to the top of the shed—to the part buried in the trees. I had chosen a short black skirt for our dinner and had not worn panties underneath in case I could catch a moment alone with Parker.

"You're leaving soon, huh?" I asked, as we got settled next to each other on the shed. I could tell he was bored at our place; the reality was that he was just passing through.

"I was going to stay longer, but Mark is so busy." His eyes were lit up. He reached out and put his hand on my thigh. "It was nice to finally meet you, Helen. Take care of him for me."

"I'll see what I can do." I moved his hand up my thigh.

"Is this a good idea?"

I scooted closer, turned around, and straddled him. He looked amused. "You know, Parker," I said, "Shelby was incredibly wrong. I fucking love your facial hair. If you shave it off, you'll be shaving off your entire being."

"Is that so?" His smile widened.

"I will dream about your facial hair forever. I can honestly say that I am in love with it."

I unzipped his pants and pulled his cock out, then buried my face in his neck, taking in his smell and tasting it, trying to bury it in my memory. He moaned and put his big hands on my waist. I slid myself onto his hard cock. I'd never forget Parker's face, his eyes, his hands, his mustache, his sideburns, and the satisfaction they had given me.

When he was coming, Parker whispered in my ear, "I won't shave them off, Helen. Just so I can fuck you again someday."

The next morning Mark and I said good-bye to Parker as he and Shelby took off. Then Mark shared some good news with me. "I finished it."

"You finished your book?"

"Yup. This morning. It's basically done."

I screamed, "Oh my God, Mark, that's so exciting!"

I kissed his cheeks and felt an unexpected stubble. He took in my quizzical look, then ran his hand over his chin and just smiled.

JEREMY EDWARDS

LE PETIT DÉJEUNER

S MUCH AS WE ENJOY getting it on at night, it is the morning that is our special time. Nighttime sex is torrid and wild. When our evening draws to an end and Lisa lands sprawling on the bed, I sometimes think her panties will evaporate into thin air from the sheer heat of her cunt.

At night, we are fuckers.

In the morning, our passion is quiet, beautiful, and intense. We are lovers.

We fell in love in Paris. Our first kiss was in front of the Eiffel Tower. Perhaps this is why we've done our best to make the apartment resemble a little corner of France, within the great city of Cleveland, Ohio. When no one is looking, we refer to the immediate neighborhood as the *arrondissement*. The bookshelves are sprinkled with Balzac and *Asterix*. Unassuming Rhône wines haunt the kitchen counter, echoing the mood of the lazy still life that freshens the living room with flowers and peaches.

The bed we share sports Continental linens, which we launder in lavender-scented detergent. The coffee whose aroma permeates our morning atmosphere is, *bien sûr,* a French Roast. Amazingly, there is an authentic *patisserie* within walking distance, and I venture there for croissants each day while Lisa bathes. As I return with the croissants she emerges, smelling like olive-oil soap in particular and delicious little French hotels in general. If there should happen to be a dusting of Great Lakes snow on the topmost pastry, I choose to imagine that it transubstantiates into confectioner's sugar as soon as the croissants and I enter Lisa's warm sphere of influence.

We always awake hungry for each other, but also just plain hungry. We breakfast from a rustic Provençal tray—at which true Parisian sophisticates would turn up their noses, but whose sunny yellow cheers us on winter days. Keeping the flaky crumbs out of the linens has long since been declared, by mutual assent, a lost cause. By now, I boast a prodigious adroitness with our handheld vacuum cleaner.

After croissants and coffee, our flesh mingles among the crisp linens. The scents of our bodies bond with the coffee and bakery aromas. I start by stroking Lisa's ass. It is firm and tastefully lewd like the peaches in the still life. She coos and wiggles, communicating the desire for my caresses. I, of course, fulfill this desire *toute suite*. I alternate between pleasuring her ass and petting her hair, her back, and her thighs, watching her tremble as she enjoys anticipating my return to her bottom. She folds her arms between her head and the pillow, relishing the passivity of being touched, and letting her ecstasy express itself through her legs only. Her muscular limbs kick with exuberant bliss; they squeeze together and release, and her toes curl and flex.

When I venture between Lisa's thighs, I feel as if I'm having dessert. Dessert with breakfast, luxury of luxuries! And when I coax her nectar down, it tastes as sweet to me as marmalade. She takes hold of my *baguette*, where a drop of *crème* has already appeared.

Where her cunt tastes like sweets, her mouth tastes like love. I want to lick and taste every inch of her, not in the raunchy way I devour her at night, but slowly, sweetly. I cup the satisfying roundness of her *derrière*, a perfect bowl, in fact, of sensuality.

And yet, no bowl bounds my conception of Lisa. She is a horizonless landscape of delicious, sustaining beauty, from the buttery freshness of her neck to the sensitive nook under each arm to the shiny daintiness of her toenails. I want to frolic atop her, squirm into her, come over her. She is a picnic in the park and the softball game afterward, a dip in the lake and a roll in the mud…the summer day that only wanes so that it may enchant you again as a summer evening. I want to be totally embraced by her love, her acceptance, her cunt, her smile. I want to pet, tickle, squeeze, lick and ride her till our nerves melt together into soup. I want to see her lips mouth *I love you* when she can no longer speak.

As we make love, I imagine that we are back in Paris. That there is a bidet in our bathroom. That people are speaking French on the sidewalk below. That around the corner is the little pharmacy where I had to resort to an earthy pantomime to indicate that I required a box of condoms. Where the pharmacist, a handsome woman of about thirty-five with dark, humorous eyes, smiled knowingly at me when I paid for them.

"Tell me about the *pharmacienne*," Lisa requested on our last night in Paris, just as I was penetrating her with bedtime vigor. "Fuck me and tell me how she looked at you." Lisa got off on the idea that the druggist had watched me as if she wanted to personally administer the dose of condoms she had provided. She still asks to hear about it some nights, three years later.

On other nights, she wants to know all about the pretty Swiss tourist across the aisle on the bus. The one that I'd noticed, out of the corner of my eye, subtly stroking her skirt while she adored a Degas nude in a gallery at the Musée d'Orsay. Lisa likes to have me relate how this art lover delicately, but deliberately, flashed her blonde sex at me as our bus bumped along the boulevard, her smirking gaze fixed on my face. As we slide together on the midnight mattress, I talk to Lisa in broken, abrupt sentences about the tourist who winked at me with her cunt.

But I digress.

The French Roast has heightened all my sensitivities. My cock strives for Lisa's body, and my cerebral synapses fire like good old American popcorn at the erotic implications of her every sensuous motion. In the faux-French Cleveland morning, the walls of Lisa's pussy absorb each of my strokes so tenderly, yet with such solidity. I feel totally supported by her intimate embrace, just as I feel completely supported by Lisa in every aspect of our life. Her cunt understands my cock the way her mind understands my own and her emotions respond with such sensitivity to my innermost needs. Pulsating inside her, I feel her so tangibly as the source of all my small and large joys.

We fell in love in Paris, but I had only an inkling of what I was falling in love with. I fell in love with her laughter and came to know her kindness. I fell in love with her acuteness and came to know her wisdom. I fell in love with her sexy ass and came to know the ineffable rapture of being clasped every morning in her transcendent feminine grip.

Ask me to describe Lisa's face, and I cannot find the words. I can no longer see her features discretely as eyes, mouth, nose, chin…all I see is the light, the personality, the embodiment of a compassionate intelligence that is my sun and my soil. I can describe Lisa no better than I can describe the sensation of water quenching my thirst, or the flavor of fresh air in my lungs. I might as well try to describe what it feels like to be a living being.

In Paris, she was pretty as a picture. Now, I rarely see her in two dimensions. Still, there are those moments when I walk into the bedroom and observe a gorgeous creature splayed for me, waiting to be touched, waiting to have her oils made to flow, waiting to absorb me and acquire me once again…and I frame Lisa in my mind like a luscious painting. A canvas, magically enough, that I can step inside.

Orgasm is inextricably associated with the aromas of coffee and pastry and lavender. In the morning, we always come slowly, writhing in down-tempo sensuality, savoring our shuddering moments together.

We are lovers. We are lovers. We are lovers this morning.

SHARING THE LOVE

A S ALWAYS, Jane looked cool and lovely, even in the ninety-seven-degree July heat. It was Wednesday, women's day at the Russian Turkish Baths on Tenth Street, and she was sitting on the steps outside waiting for me. She was wearing a sleeveless, bright orange sheath dress that contrasted stunningly with her short violet hair.

"I'm so glad you called me," she said, "and I'm so glad you dumped Adrian."

"I *had* to dump him," I answered. "How could I go on with him after I found out he was poking that Carmen? I can't believe how he tried to laugh it off, saying she meant nothing to him. Does he think I'm an idiot?" My voice had got all shrill as the anger flooded over me.

"It's funny, this is the first time we've been to the baths together even though we both love the baths and we've been coming here for years," Jane said, wisely changing the subject. "And," she continued,

"It's great to go to the sauna in the middle of a heat wave, because after the sauna, you come outside and you're cool all day long."

We went upstairs, through the entrance, and into the reception room, left our valuables at the desk and got the keys to a couple of lockers. In the locker room, we stripped off our clothes. Jane turned to face me, naked as a newborn. "I want to tell you," she said, "I never liked Adrian, the way he was always shooting his mouth off about who had just published him. He was always bragging about what a big banana he was. I bet his banana isn't big at all."

I started to laugh, how did she know? When I asked her, she said, grinning, "I didn't know. I was just trying to get you smiling."

I glanced down and saw a jumble of colors—purples and reds and blues—right between her legs where her crotch hairs should be. It was a tattoo of a heart: a big red heart outlined in purple with a purple arrow through it. Inscribed inside the heart in Gothic script, I could make out the letter J, an ampersand, and the letter G.

G, I immediately knew, was Jane's longtime live-in sweetheart George.

"How romantic," I said. "You have a Valentine between your legs."

"Yes," she answered, "Georgie has one also, on his arm, only his says G & J. We got them on our first anniversary. I was going to put mine on my arm too, but then I decided this was a much better place." She placed her hand over the tattoo and rubbed it as if for good luck. "We love each other so much," she said. "We have a perfect understanding. Together we can do anything...anything," she repeated and then she winked at me. "Last month we got engaged. Now look at this." She sat down on the locker-room bench, spread her legs and opened herself with her delicate fingers.

"Come on," she said. "Take a look, don't be shy." I stepped between her legs, bent my head down close. I could smell her, her bitter wine cunt smell mixed with patchouli. A little gold barbell was piercing her pretty, plump clit, a tiny diamond embedded in each end.

"George and I got pierced together. He got a Prince Albert with a diamond in it," she said.

"I guess you won't be able to show your engagement rings to your family," I replied.

"Maybe I will," Jane grinned. "They're very progressive."

We went downstairs to the sauna rooms and then into the Russian sauna room. The big concrete room has three tiers of long benches built into the walls. At regular intervals along the walls, buckets hung from spigots that were constantly running, filling the buckets with cold water. I loved upending the buckets, dumping the cold water over my head. It was still early and we were the only ones there. We sat next to each other on the wooden planks that constituted the benches. It felt so good to just let the heat take me, to surrender my sadness and fury to the ancient fires of the sauna gods.

I imagined that I was sitting on a rock by a stream cutting through a steamy tropical jungle. A fearless explorer wearing a pith helmet and nothing else came striding through the trees that bordered the stream and then…then… Jane interrupted my delightful reverie.

"This is the best thing we could possibly have done today," she said. She stood, and lifted a bucket off the spigot. She took a few steps forward so as not to splash me as she upended the bucket over her head. Her lovely white buns wiggled slightly as she moved.

"You look so good now," she said as she sat down again. "No more knit brows, no more frown lines. You look all fresh and sweet."

"I feel better. The sauna always does it for me."

"Me too," Jane answered, "but the heat makes me all sexed up. Whenever I get out of the sauna, the first thing I want to do is go home and jump Georgie. You ought to come over and hang out with us. We'd really cheer you up. He's always liked you; he thinks you're a great person."

I was taken aback at this sudden invitation. I never had much luck with threesomes plus I didn't know if I was ready to jump into bed with my adventurous friends.

I finally said, "Do you two do this often—invite playmates over to cavort with you?"

"Not all that often," Jane answered. "Only when we feel like it. We have so much love, acres and acres of love, miles and miles. There's plenty to share. Like John Lennon said, 'the love you take is equal to the love you make.' "

"Right," I said, still nonplused, "but I just don't think I'm cool enough for anything like that."

Jane jumped up, grabbed a water bucket and dumped the water over my head.

"You will be, you will be," she chanted.

I pretended to be annoyed. "Very funny," I said in a sarcastic tone, but the icy water did make my skin tingle in a delicious way. When we parted an hour later outside the sauna, Jane said, "I hope I didn't make you uncomfortable in there. I was trying to show you that Georgie and I would love to share our love with you. Please think about it."

"Sure," I told her.

I walked over to St. Marks Place, to Puerto Rico Coffee and Spice, to get a pound of the Organic French Peruvian Coffee I like so much. The cute clerk who measured out my coffee had a graceful, rangy build; long thighs like pistons, just like Adrian's. Suddenly he looked just like Adrian. He gave me a big smile when he handed me my bag of coffee, but I didn't smile back. I couldn't wait to get away from him; I grabbed my coffee and dashed out of there.

That night, I couldn't fall asleep. Although I had changed the sheets twice since we split, I thought I could smell Adrian on them, his smell of butterscotch and Parliament Lights. When I closed my eyes, I saw the smiling face of the clerk in the coffee shop, then Adrian's face, then his whole fine body, his big mule dick. I tossed and turned and finally realized I'd never get any sleep until I soothed my aching cooch. I got my beloved old blue rabbit vibrator from the bed table drawer and lubed it up. But just at the moment of truth, just as I was about to come, I saw Adrian above me, grinning down like a Cheshire cat.

I promised myself I'd call Jane and George first thing in the morning.

Jane picked up the phone. When I told her about my decision, she said, "Wonderful. Can you come Thursday? Eight thirty? I'll make dinner."

That's only two nights away, I thought, and then I realized I was scared. Would I be able to please my two sexually sophisticated friends? Would they be able to please me? Was this really how they expressed their love, by sharing it, or were they just bored? I felt like hanging up the phone and running away, but I made myself say, "Okay. Eight thirty is fine."

Two nights later, I found myself climbing the six flights to their loft on Crosby Street, nervously clutching the bottle of champagne I had brought.

In response to my timid knock, the door was flung open immediately and there stood George. He was wearing white linen trousers and a white T-shirt that said SLUT on it. He was barefoot and grinning, his shaved head shining. He grabbed me in a big bear hug. "Hi, tiger," he said. Surprisingly, I didn't mind his arms around me. "Well, look at you," he said. "You look like the femme fatale you are. Jane made sushi. I hope you're hungry."

I told him I was and handed him the bottle of champagne.

"Perfect," he said. "We love bubbly."

I followed him into their large loft. The table in front of the windows was set for three, a big bottle of plum wine at the center. Jane was moving about in the kitchen area. "Hi babe," she called out to me. In the far corner, their big bed was covered with a colorful patchwork quilt. My eyes were drawn to it, but I quickly looked away.

We decided to save the champagne for later. Soon we were sitting around the table, our glasses filed with plum wine, a platter of tuna rolls and a platter of sashimi in front of us. The tuna rolls looked like little pussies with frilly pink labia to me and the sashimi looked like stubby little pricks. I wondered if Jane and George were thinking the same thing because there was an awkward silence between us.

"Are you two thinking what I'm thinking?" I asked.

"You mean that the tuna rolls look like little cunts?" said Jane.

"Exactly," I answered, relieved. I wasn't the only one with a filthy mind.

"I wasn't thinking that," George said, "although now that you mention it, they do. I was thinking that these kinds of arrangements can be awkward and, you know, we don't have to do anything. We can just eat and drink and talk. We love your company. We don't want you to feel pressured," he concluded.

I thought about what he'd said. "I don't know if I'm feeling pressured," I said, "maybe just nervous."

"Well then," said George, "why don't we just change locale, move to where it's more comfortable. Let's sit on the sofa."

In a few minutes, I was sitting between them, our food in front of us on the glass-topped coffee table. Jane had brought over the bottle of plum wine and refilled our glasses.

The sushi was delicious; we finished everything on the platters. There was a bit of wine left and I divided that between us.

"How did you two meet?" I asked.

"Actually, he picked me up in a supermarket," Jane said.

"Oh, no, no," said George. "*She* picked me up."

"Uh-uh," Jane corrected him. "It was you who came over to me in the vegetable section and wanted to know if the avocado you were holding was ripe enough."

George shook his head. "No, no, it was *you* holding the avocado," he said. They both started laughing and then, leaning over me, their mouths met in a long kiss.

"Let's not forget our guest," Jane said, when they broke the kiss. All at once they were both on me, kissing my cheeks, my neck, my shoulders. "We love you," Jane whispered in my ear.

"Indeed," said George, "we do. May we seduce you?" He was leaning toward me, and I could feel his erection, warm and promising, pushing against my thigh.

"Yes," I said. "Yes."

Jane unbuttoned my blouse and slipped it off. George removed my bra. "Boobs like a goddess," he said softly.

"When I saw them in the sauna," Jane added, "this is what I wanted to do." She bent her head and fastened her Cupid's bow lips delicately around a nipple. She nibbled that nipple like it was made of candy. George took my other tit in his big, hungry mouth, gobbling and sucking. It felt divine.

Jane lifted her head. "This is how we share our love," she said. George released my other tit.

"Shall we move to the bed?" he suggested. I nodded, and in a minute, I was lying on my back on their big soft bed. My friends took off the rest of my clothes and began to touch me. I had four hands stroking my belly, my pussy, my ass, my tits. My body was waltzing beneath their loving fingers. I opened my legs wide to show them my little candy box.

"You're beautiful everywhere," said George. He peeled off his shirt and pants. He had nothing underneath and his bulbous red cock, the head intersected by the Prince Albert I'd been told about, pointed right between my legs. He started to stroke it. "I want to get as big as I can for you, ladies," he said. "Dear Jane, now please take off your dress." She pulled off her dress; she wasn't wearing any underwear either. She paraded before us. The heart tattoo on her vulva looked like an exotic flower. She did a little bump and grind, then she spread her pink pussy open to show off her diamond clit ring. George licked his lips and

I thought how pretty her pussy looked with the diamond ring on top like a crown.

"You know what I'd like," said George. "I'd like to see you two lovelies kiss."

Willingly, I opened my arms and Jane fell on top of me, her body covering mine like a silk-gloved hand. I put my arm around her and we tumbled over on the bed. My hands played with her soft ass. Her fingers stroked my back, as she fucked my mouth with her plum-wine tongue. I could feel the silver ring in her clit tap, tap, tapping against my labia. I got so aroused I started to jerk my hips to and fro in the ancient dance of desire.

Suddenly, I felt George's hand between my legs, between Jane and me. He was lifting her up, using his hand as a wedge. Then I felt the heavy heat, the weight of his sex as it moved into me, moving in and out. I opened wider, wanting him even deeper, but then he pulled out of me and started pumping into Jane. I watched as he slid in and out of her juicy slit. It excited me even more so that when he stopped diddling Jane and penetrated me again I was in ecstasy. Back and forth he went, bringing the three of us moaning and yelling into the biggest orgasm I could remember.

We lay together in a happy sweaty heap.

"Now's the time for the champagne," Jane said.

If *this* was sharing the love, I'd do it anytime.

MICHAEL HEMMINGSON

TOYS

AFTER WORK, I went to Rosina's apartment. Her front door was unlocked, like she had told me it would be. I could hear her in her bedroom, typing away at her computer. She was sitting at her desk in shorts and a halter, hair pulled up in a messy tail.

"Hey," I said.

She spun around in her chair. "You!"

"Expecting someone else?" I sat on the bed.

"Only you. Only you would be here."

"What are you writing?"

"What does it look like?"

I saw a poem on the screen. "What's the subject?"

"Flying. If I had wings," she said, "I could fly. I could fly here—I could fly there. I'd be rich! Everyone in the world marveling at how I can *fly.*"

"*I* can fly." I lay back on the bed.

Rosina got on top of me. She tickled me and said, "Can you now?"

"Stop!"

"No."

She stopped.

"I'm a superhero," I told her. "But this is a secret. Well, now you know the secret. When I'm a superhero, I can fly. I'm a superhero—with no name."

"Show me," she said. She kissed my nose. "I want to see you fly."

"Can't," I said. "Not in costume. Right now, I'm a regular person."

"But when you're a superhero—?"

"I can fly."

"Well," Rosina said, "not *all* of them can."

"Superman does."

"Batman doesn't."

"He doesn't have superpowers. He's a vigilante."

"Batman is *sexy,*" she said, and rolled off me, looking at the ceiling. "I've seen those movies. I'm not talking about the goofy Batman on TV. I mean the movies, *armor-plated nipples and everything!*"

"All superheroes are sexy," I said, bored.

"Does Spiderman fly?"

"No. He swings around the city with his fake webs."

"Who's that guy who runs really fast?"

"The Flash."

She said, "I'd like to be like that, run around all in red, running faster than—faster than I don't know what."

I moved to kiss her, to say, "You're Wonder Woman."

She got up. "No. I'm too short, if you have not noticed. So," she bent down and grabbed my legs, "when you're a superhero, do you wear one of those tight, sexy spandex outfits?"

"You bet."

"And battle evil foes?" Her hands were running up my legs.

"I keep the world safe and clean," I told her.

"Sexy hero," she said, unzipping my pants. She took my cock out, and started sucking on it. She sucked long and slow; I relaxed and allowed myself to enjoy this. I came, but she didn't swallow. She let it go out of her mouth and down my cock. She looked at it. She moved up onto the bed and put her head on my chest. "So where are we going with all this?"

"This?"

"This," she said, touching my stomach, "and this," touching my wet cock, covered in saliva and semen.

"This." I touched her back, her ass.

She turned and kissed my neck, nuzzled it with her face. "You smell good."

"You smell pretty good yourself."

"You always smell like sex," Rosina said. "Is this a good or bad thing?"

"Everything between us is a good thing," I said.

"Everything just seems to be *too* good. We'll end in tragedy," she said.

"Tears?"

"Violence?"

"Pain?"

"Maybe blood," she said. She sat up. "Put your hands here," she said, indicating her neck. She took my hands, and put them around her neck. "There, there. Now choke me."

"Why?"

"I want you to."

"I don't know how."

"Keep your hands there and *squeeze.*"

"Like this?"

"Harder."

"I'll hurt you."

"Just do it, you bastard."

I squeezed her neck. "You like this?"

"You know what I like?" She broke free from me. She plopped down on her hands and knees, body on top of me. She said, "What I really like is for men to fuck me from behind, my ass high in the air, and reach over, here, *here*"—taking my hand—"reach over like so and choke me like so as they fuck me from behind like so."

"Is this romantic talk?"

"Depends on your upbringing," Rosina said.

"Sometimes," I said, "I like the silence."

She put her head on my chest. "Is this getting serious?"

We stopped talking, and started kissing, which led to fucking. I fucked her the way she wanted, my cock in her pussy from behind, and I reached over and choked her. It wasn't an easy thing to do; I thought it'd be easier if she were on her back, I'd have better access to her neck. "Choke me harder," she pleaded, and I did, and her body shook as she came, my hand still at her neck. "Oh boy," she said.

I began to enter Rosina's world of pain: her delight.

I was touching, caressing her breasts. I pinched her nipples, which were hard; I pinched lightly.

"Pinch them harder," she said.

I did.

"Harder," she said.

I was afraid I'd hurt her.

"I want the pain," she said. "It makes me horny."

She gave an example. She got up, found a pair of clothespins in a cabinet in the kitchen, and placed a clothespin on each nipple. With the clamping down on each nipple, she took in a deep, hissing breath.

"Fuck," she said.

"You like that," I said.

"Yes yes," she said. "Take them off."

I did, quickly.

"Put them back on."

I did, and this time I took delight in watching the pins squeeze into her flesh.

"Ahh, fuck," she said.

I took one off.

"Now use your fingers."

I took the nipple in question between two fingers.

"Squeeze," she said.

I squeezed.

I started to become quite good at choking her while we fucked, whether she was on her belly or on her knees. Repetition makes you better. I also started to enjoy this activity. I was never quite sure if it was mental or physical for Rosina, but as long as it got her off and made her happy, it made me happy.

We started biting one another, soft at first, then harder, sometimes until we drew blood from each other's punctured flesh, fragile as anything in the universe. The biting was not just into the body, but into the soul.

"I have something," Rosina said, standing naked before me.

"Yeah?"

"Something I want you to use on me," she said.

She went to her closet, and produced a cat-o'-nine-tails. I'd seen such a flogging device in magazines, in movies.

"Where'd you get that?" I asked.

"I've had it awhile," Rosina said. "I want you to use it on me," she said.

It was black and ominous. She handed it to me. She lay on her stomach, on the bed. "Use it on my back," she told me. "Use it on my ass, my legs."

I did so, lightly, uncertain.

"It's okay to start off soft," she said, "but increase your strength. Gradually. I want you to get to a point where you could almost make me bleed."

I did this. I hit her with the cat-o'-nine-tails just as she said: her back, her ass, her legs. She seemed to like it best on her ass. I started to get into it. I started hitting her harder, enjoying the smack of leather against flesh. Harder. She began to cry out with each blow. Tears in her eyes. She wanted more. Welts were beginning to form on her ass, the backs of her legs. I concentrated on her back, 'til welts formed there.

"Okay," she said. *"Stop."*

I stopped. I, too, was almost out of breath.

"Now get on me," she said. "Fuck me, I can't stand it, fuck me!"

I entered her from behind, I reached over to choke her. We fucked for a bit, then she turned around and put her legs on my shoulders.

"Slap me," she said.

I raised a hand.

"Slap me."

Fucking her, I slapped her, hard, across the face.

She just looked at me, some blood on her lip. "Not that hard," she said.

"I'm sorry," I said, reaching down and licking the blood away.

"Slap me again," she said.

I did, but not as hard.

Rosina bought toys several days a week, usually at thrift stores, sometimes at the toy store. She loved her children's toys.

But she had adult toys hidden under her bed, and it wasn't until we'd been seeing each other for a month that she brought them all out, and wanted to share them with me.

Anal beads, large double-headed black dildos, a dog collar, other assorted rubber penetrating devices. While Rosina liked the beads or my fingers in her ass, she didn't care for anal sex all that much. She wasn't into ass-licking, piss, or even swallowing my come. She liked pain, she liked to whack her clit off, she liked me to choke her. It was easy to get into what she enjoyed, as I got into any woman's pleasure, however alien it was to me. I adapted well.

The image I have of her—this image will always stay with me—is of Rosina surrounded by her toys, a milieu of toys: the toys she liked to buy and play with, fill the empty spaces of the apartment with.

This is what I knew about her—or this could've been mere assumption—and the image of her that sticks like hot glue to the fingertips of my reverie is Rosina as I saw her one night, when I went to her apartment and she had bought a bag full of magnetic letters, the colored alphabet letters I seem to recall having played with when I was a very small person. "Look! Look!" she said with glee, like a small person, and she said, "Help me with them," an invitation to play. She tore open the plastic bag the colored letters were contained in; they scattered across the floor of her kitchen like stupid human dreams forever lost in a car crash. She went to her knees, told me to come to her: play, help, fight. She started putting the letters on the white refrigerator, where she had a color print of a happy smiley-face woman with large eyes and the caption HOME HONEY, I'M HIGH and two postcards, one of a brunette holding a gun and shooting, another of a man with a gun, an image from the movie *Reservoir Dogs*. There was a mixture of delight and anxiety on her face; she looked at me and said, "Won't you help me?" I got to my knees, picked up several letters, started putting them on the fridge with her. The kitchen was hot (like the rest of the apartment) and I felt very sad. She must've seen something on my face because she said, "You think this is silly, you don't like doing this."

"No," I said, "there's nothing silly about this," and so we were like two children frantically picking up the alphabet from her floor—letters that I thought would any moment now get up and dance—sticking them to the door of the fridge. Merriment, yes, a small one's joy on her small triangular face; and when I looked at the kitchen table that held a lot of other toys, used and new, I felt sad again; I knew there was something missing. Something was missing from her past (something was missing from mine) and something was missing between us, yet another space to be filled, a vacuous interior needing intestines.

"You buy so many toys," I said. I sat down at the table and played with a dinosaur.

Rosina looked at her letters, arranged them in a way she liked better. "Yes, I do," she said.

She sat in my lap like she always did, arms around my neck and looking down at me with her dark eyes, dark circles under her eyes—my face pressed against her breasts, the smell of her now on me, that smell that was not perfume but some men's cologne I'd never heard of that mixed well with her skin and gave her the smell I knew I'd forever associate with her, an invasion of my psyche: my memory of Rosina.

She kissed me on the lips, she kissed me on the forehead. "Just think," she said, "I keep collecting more and more toys, we'll never have to buy toys for our children."

One night at her apartment I felt, for the first time, like I did not belong there. I was feeling weak. All day I had had this sensation of horror, but all I wanted was to be with her, to hold her, to have her hold me, to play with her toys, to talk, to have her warm body against mine, to make love, to do anything, anything but be away from her; whip her, slap her, beat her, choke her. Her apartment was dark, candles were lit all around, flamenco guitar music on the CD player. She was in the bathroom, hair pinned up, applying makeup in a way she never had before, looking at herself in the mirror; and when I went into the bathroom, her eyes on me, from the reflection, were eyes of rancor. She seemed angry, like she didn't want me there; she seemed evil in the candlelight. I tried to kiss her and she pushed me away. Once, she told me she did a lot of symbolic things, some abstruse and some subtle, and I would have to get used to it. "Like this band on my wedding finger," she said, "is to remind me who and what I'm really married to: *myself*, I'm married to myself; and this necklace, these earrings in the shape of hearts, to remind me to always follow my heart."

"Why are you here with me?" she had asked after we made love the night before. "I don't understand," she said.

I grabbed her necklace and said, "I'm just following my heart."

In the candlelit apartment she told me she was having second thoughts; she wasn't sure if she wanted a partner, someone to tell her to come to bed at four a.m. while she was working on a poem; someone to tell her to eat; someone to even talk to, to be present for, to remind herself of herself. "I'm used to being a hermit," she said. "I like being a hermit." I told her I would go but she grabbed me and said no and we held each other and I smelled her and I was all the more confused.

I saw her touching herself, making herself come, the way she liked to, lying on her stomach, and how hard she did this to herself, finger to clit. When I tried doing it to her, I never seemed to do it hard or fast enough. "Press, press," she said, her body drenched in light, sweet-smelling sweat.

As I saw her masturbating, the image was replaced again by that of her on the kitchen floor, picking up the alphabet, playing with her toys.

Yes, it was over and I would live with this hole in my heart forever, and I'd never look at toys the same way again.

An Ordinary Love

AH, YES. I enjoy tormenting my wife, Sasha. I do it because she lets me. Sasha lets me torment her because she enjoys it. We play little games, share mutual fetishes. She likes watching me chop onions before I fuck her over the kitchen counter so that she can taste their bite and cry without cause. I like watching her humiliate herself for me. There is a balance between us. "Andrew," she'll say, while we're sitting next to each other on the train, on the way to work. There's always urgency in her voice and I know what she's going to say before the words fall from her mouth. I'll turn to look at her, then look away, quietly observing the other passengers—the way the man across the aisle from us adjusts himself when he thinks no one is looking, the way the woman in the row in front of us keeps jerking her head, trying to stay awake.

While I'm watching all this, I'll turn toward her, slide my hand across my left thigh to Sasha's right, squeezing gently, slipping my fingers beneath the hem of her skirt. She'll clear her throat and look out the opposite window at the passing scenery, a light pink blush spreading across her face. She'll pretend to be somewhat disturbed. But she'll brush her thumb across my wrist, and lean closer into me. We'll stare at each other in these moments, and the rest of the world recedes. All I see is my wife, her legs spreading ever wider as we pass New Rochelle.

Later, always, I smell her on my wedding ring.

Sasha enjoys these torments because she appreciates the view from the bottom. She told me this on our third date. She was kneeling on the floor of my apartment, smiling up at me on the couch, my pants around my ankles. "I don't care what you think of me," she said, with a little laugh. "I like the view from down here." And with that, she swallowed the length of my cock, continuing to laugh. I could feel the vibrations of her throat muscles. It was a curious sensation.

Sasha carries her secrets in tight knots along her spine. When she's lying in bed, her back facing me, I can see their outlines in the dark. Sometimes, I reach for her to trace them with my fingertips. She shrinks away, curling herself tightly. I withdraw but continue to watch. Sometimes, after we've shared a bottle of wine and we're on the couch watching television, she'll dance around her secrets, try to share a part of herself, but she never gets too far. I don't push. I don't want to complicate the games we play with history.

We married after dating for only seven months. I proposed to her after a free jazz concert in Central Park. We were sitting on a bench, where she was trembling and smoking a cigarette. It was cold and windy and miserable. I put my coat around her shoulders, knowing it would smell like tobacco for weeks afterward. It was not a moment. I didn't make promises I couldn't keep. But after I asked and showed her the ring, she took a long drag on her cigarette and answered, "I'm going to say yes because I think you have the capacity to hurt me the way I need you to."

People think they know Sasha. When they see her, they think she is a slender, cheerful young woman who is always in a good mood. I see Sasha with her arms bound behind her back so tightly that her elbows are touching. There is anger in her eyes and her lips are swollen. She is seated on a wooden chair, her breasts thrust forward, a thin silver chain between her nipples. I am standing, one foot on the chair between her thighs, only a few inches away from her cunt. She looks right through me as she tries to inch forward, create a point of contact between us. I simply smile.

Sasha wants me to taker her somewhere—a place she has no vocabulary for—a place neither of us has been. I can hear it in her cries when we're fucking, or I'm stretching her limbs across our bed, or we're crammed into the antiseptic space of the train bathroom. I can always tell that we're not quite there yet. It creates tension between us. Tonight, I wait for Sasha to return home from work. She is late, as usual. I never know where she goes after work. I don't ask. I am in our backyard listening to the night when I feel her cool hands on my shoulders. Without turning around, I say, "You're late."

"I know," she replies and returns to the house.

I finger my belt buckle, and stand, slowly. I find Sasha in our bathroom, undressing. She smiles at my reflection in the mirror, unraveling her hair from the two platinum hair sticks she uses to sweep her hair up most days. When she sets them on the counter, the sound echoes through the room. She quietly slips out of her dress and I glance at the scars along her upper back—scars for which she offers no explanation. Lower, there are scars that I have given her.

The thin, slightly braided scar just above the crack of her ass, that runs the width of her back, I gave to her in Miami. We were staying in one of those boutique hotels in South Beach. We came back to our room after a night of strolling Collins Avenue, drinking mojitos, dancing to *la musica Cubana,* pretending we were people different from ourselves. She quickly undressed, splashed some water on her face and crawled into bed with my straight razor. She crossed one leg over the other, the tip of the open razor pressed into her knee. "I once saw this movie," she said, trailing her hand along the empty space next to her.

I knelt at her feet, pressing my lips against the exposed soft spot of her inner ankle. I slid my hands up her muscled calf, slightly gritty with sand. She uncrossed her legs. I lay atop her, letting her feel the full weight of my body. Sasha's chest tightened, her breathing grew labored. I kissed her, roughly, sliding my tongue into her mouth, across her teeth. I freed the razor from her grip, set it on the pillow next to her face. My hands, still rough with sand, slid between our bodies, up her torso, around the outer curves of her breasts. She arched upward and I moved my lips to her neck, tugging at the taut skin with my teeth until she gasped, loudly.

I turned Sasha onto her stomach and lay next to her, one of my legs draped over hers, my mouth at her ear, whispering to her about all the things I would do to her that night and every night thereafter. I called her the names she likes to be called—whore, slut, mine. I took the razor and slid the dull edge along her spine and across her back, navigating the tightly knotted secrets and scars. I stopped just above her ass, pressed the sharp edge of the razor at one end of her back and quickly drew it across. She hissed as tiny droplets of blood appeared. I tossed the razor aside, and inched her thighs further apart. We had seen the same movie. I raised her ass toward me and slid my cock inside her. It seemed like all the muscles in her body tensed. She reached back without ceremony, digging her nails into my skin, urging me deeper. Afterward, I told her I loved her, the way I always did. I touched the drying blood. She sat up, wrapped the sheet around herself and lit a cigarette. I watched the silhouette of smoke curl around her. Sasha, a longtime Johnny Cash fan, smiled at me and whispered, "Love is a burning thing."

I want to know the stories of all her scars, but I'm not sure I'm willing to pay the price for that knowledge. Sasha continues to stare at my reflection. She is an expert at holding a gaze. She won't break—not for anything. She's that way about many things. She turns around and leans back against the bathroom counter. I pull my belt free from my waist and wrap it around her throat. She arches an eyebrow, feigns boredom. Sasha is very good at pushing buttons.

I cast my eyes downward and she reaches forward, unzips my slacks, slides a hand into my boxers. Her touch is cold and I shiver as she begins sliding her hand up and down along the length of my cock. She is neither gentle nor rough. My jaw clenches and I clear my throat. I don't want to give her the satisfaction of knowing how much I enjoy her touch. When Sasha brushes her lips across the tip of my cock, before wrapping them around, flicking her tongue against the wet slit,

I stop her, push her away. It is a rough, unkind gesture. Still holding the end of my belt, I start walking away. When there's a tug, she starts to crawl after me, tentatively at first, then faster to keep up.

When I stop at the foot of our bed and turn to look at her, she is less smug than she was before. "You have not come close," she says.

"To what?"

"You'll know when you get there." She sits cross-legged, waiting for my next move. We are, I think, very large chess pieces. I cup her chin with my hand, pulling her mouth open. She tilts her head back, her hands holding my ass as I begin to slide my cock in and out of her mouth with slow, deliberate thrusts. Every now and again, she closes her mouth slightly, letting her teeth graze against my shaft. I slide my fingers through her dark hair, closing them into tight fists. Sasha brings one of her hands to my balls and grabs them between her fingers, grasping as tightly as I have hold of her. I grunt, try to twist away, but her grip is steady and unforgiving. I thrust harder, faster. She makes muffled coughing sounds. After I come, I stagger. Sasha wipes her lips with one thumb. She swallows. She waits for my next move. I'm not sure, but I think I hear her say "Check."

Sasha hates having her pussy licked. Nothing gets her angrier than when I tie her down and lie between her thighs, lavishing my tongue across her swollen pussy lips and hard nub of a clit. She won't speak to me for days afterward. When pressed, she says that it bores her and lacks purpose. But she comes when I put my mouth on her and it's the only time she makes any real sounds—high-pitched moans that she utters at a staccato pace. I pull her onto the bed and slide my hands up her inner thighs. The muscles flex. I press my forehead against the mound of her pussy, breathing heavily. She smacks my forehead, but I push her arms away, sliding my tongue inside her cunt before drawing it up toward her clit. Sasha digs her heels into my back, just beneath my shoulder blades, far harder than necessary. When I look up, I see her head turned to the side, tears of anger threatening to spill over the crests of her eyelids.

"Do I have you where you want me to have you?"

"Fuck you," Sasha says. It is a wonder she can get words out through teeth clenched so tightly. I thrust two fingers inside of her, deep and hard. She winces. I slide my fingers out, then drag them up her body, between her breasts, leaving a damp trail. I straddle her waist, squeezing her breasts together. There will be bruises here. I reach over to the night table, and fumble for a pair of handcuffs. Defiantly, Sasha throws her arms above her head. I clasp the cuffs around each wrist. Sasha shrugs. I slide off the bed and tell her I'll be back. I wait in the hallway just outside our bedroom. I can hear frustration in her breathing. She mutters unkind things about me.

I go to the den and turn on the television, loud, letting her hear it. Twenty minutes later, I hear footsteps. "Now, we have a problem," I say. She stands in the doorway, her hands cuffed in front of her. She looks lonely, abandoned. She is beautiful. I stand and quickly close the distance between us. Clasping her throat with one hand, I force her against the wall. I smack her face, once, then reach down between her legs where she is wet. I turn her around and kick her legs apart. One of her cheeks is pressed against the wall, her eyes are tightly shut. I rub my hand across her ass, pulling my fingers along the cleft before smacking that ass once, twice. She makes no sound. I smack her again, hard enough that the palm of my hand tingles. She stands on the tips of her toes, offering herself to me. I spank her until my arm is heavy and the muscles in my shoulder burn. We are both sweating. She is raw. Strands of her hair are plastered against her face. When I scratch her reddened ass, it leaves white streaks.

This time, when I slide my cock inside her pussy, she moans, loudly. "That's fucking right," I tell her. I call her my bitch and tell her I want to hear just how much she wants this. She raises her arms over her head, her cuffed fists resting against the wall. To every question I ask, she gives me the answer I want to hear. I twist her nipples with the fingers of one hand, and stroke her clit in tight, fast circles with the fingers of the other. Her head rocks from side to side. I want to overwhelm her with stimulation. We are loud and vulgar. Our damp bodies come together and fall apart with sharp sucking sounds. She is liquid heat around me and I want to reach into the marrow of her with my lips, my fingers, my cock. In moments like these, her rough edges fade. Her arrogance retreats. Her body feels incredibly small and fragile. She is truly mine. I sink my teeth into her left shoulder, biting through the sweat and skin, then circling my tongue over the indentations. I kiss the back of her neck, and slow the rhythm of my hips.

Suddenly, I want to be gentle with her. As if she can sense what I'm thinking, Sasha says "Don't," her voice hoarse, almost trapped. The tension in her body begins to slacken. When she comes, I can feel her pussy pulsing around my cock. Her body heaves with sobs and slowly, she falls to the floor. I look down at her, stroking my cock. She is clearly tired, but she knows what to do. Her face shines, her lips are slightly parted. This is my way of marking her, staining her with my seed in silver streaks across her face. And when I am spent, I am the one leaning against the wall. She lies at my feet, bent and slightly broken, her arms wrapped around my legs. I touch the top of her head. Before long, I will help her up, carry her to bed.

We share an ordinary love.

Kate Laurie

My Sometimes Girlfriend

ALEXIS NEVER LETS ME PICK HER UP. That's one of her rules. Instead, she always arranges to meet me at some new restaurant or café in the next city. That's rule number two. She refuses to go anywhere in town, and she refuses to go to the same place twice. Instead I always have to drive the twenty or thirty miles to one of the neighboring cities. It's a pain, but I would do almost anything for her. Scratch that—I would do anything.

Waiting for her taxi to arrive has always been difficult. All of my insecurities come bubbling up and I wonder every time if she'll actually show, or if this is the night that she'll end it, end us. Tonight, I smoke my cigarette with shallow, impatient pulls. I check my watch for the third time. She's late. As usual.

Finally, a beat-up taxi pulls up to the curb and my heart starts racing. God, I hope it's her. The driver walks out and around to open up the back door. A grin breaks across my face; I'm almost certain that it's her now. He opens the door and an angel exits. Soft blonde curls frame a slender face. Her lips sparkle with a pink lip gloss that matches her dress. A white lace choker circles her lovely neck. She looks like a porcelain doll. While she attempts to adjust the frilly skirt of her dress, I pay the taxicab driver. I want him to leave. The looks he keeps shooting her are testing my patience. He glances at my girlfriend one last time and then pulls away from the restaurant slowly, as if he regrets having to depart.

"You look stunning, Alexis." I whisper it against her ear and take advantage of the closeness to breathe in her scent. She smells of vanilla and strawberries. I feel myself begin to harden, and I swallow the excess moisture in my mouth.

"Thank you." She blushes prettily and holds a gloved hand against her pink cheek.

I grasp that hand and lead her slowly to the restaurant's entrance. The host sees us approach and holds the door open. He opens his mouth, but forgets to greet us. Alexis has that affect on people.

I pull her seat out for her and wait patiently as she settles the layers of her dress around her. I can hear people at the surrounding tables whispering. They wonder if she's an actress, or maybe on her way to a costume party. Either way they agree that the look suits her. I smile as I look down at her. They're right. This look does suit her.

The dress looks like it belongs on some aristocrat's daughter. The pink and white jacquard fabric is edged by thick white lace around the square neck and where the tight sleeves end at her elbows. The full skirt splits in the front and another white skirt can be seen underneath. She looks like a painting come to life.

She smiles shyly at me and I can hear the man seated behind us gasp. I fight the urge to glare at him and instead sit down across from her. Our waiter rushes to our table to see what he can get us. I order a glass of red wine. She demurely declines. She's not here for food or drink. She has only come here to be admired. I know this, but I try not to let it bother me. I know that the lustful glances and whispered admiration feed a secret part of her that only I understand. It's one of our dirty secrets. I glance away as my jaw tightens. We have so many of those.

Later, I nurse my glass of wine and pick at the meal I ordered. I'm not hungry, but this isn't the type of place where you can just order drinks. Every once in a while, Alexis leans forward to dab at my lips daintily with her napkin. I doubt I have anything on them, but when I see the jealous stares I understand. I decide to feed her ego and lean forward to gently cup a rosy cheek as I mutter my thanks against her hand. She blushes again and I hear someone's fork hit the ground. The joy and triumph I see in her eyes makes me feel like the luckiest man in the world.

She gives me a discreet nod. She is ready to leave. I raise my hand and the overly solicitous waiter immediately rushes forward to take my credit card. It always amazes me what better service I get when I am with her. I sign the slip and pull her chair out for her. As soon as she stands, I offer her my arm. As we leave, I can almost feel the desperate patrons trying to catch one last glimpse of her. She can feel it too. I can tell by the way her hand grips my arm just a bit tighter and her breath quickens.

I open the car door for her and then lean down to make sure that all of the fabric of her skirt is inside. She runs her hand up my inner thigh. I try unsuccessfully to hide my grin. Oh yes, she enjoyed the attention tonight. I quickly get into my car and start the engine. As I drive toward our destination her hands teasingly touch my body. Whenever we hit a red light, she pulls back and sits demurely once again. She's ready for the driver in the neighboring vehicle to admire her.

I feel a familiar bittersweet pain in my chest as we reach the hotel. I try to decide if my heart is breaking or just overjoyed as the clerk hands us a key. He grins at us knowingly and I want to smash his face in. He's been on duty the last few times we have come here. He's realized what our meetings are really about. We will have to find another place next time.

I have barely locked the door before my demure girlfriend is replaced by a wanton vixen. Her gloved hands rip my shirt from my pants and are already busy trying to yank my belt from my waist. I grip her wrists to stop the frantic motions and her gorgeous blue eyes look up at me. God, she is beautiful. I lean down and place a gentle kiss upon her mouth. Her lips open and we share a rare intimate kiss. I smile against her damp mouth. So that's where the strawberry scent was coming from.

As much as I want to just hold her and gently love her I know that isn't what she wants. I remove my hands from her wrists and instead help her remove my pants. The hungry look on her face is almost frightening. I step out of my pants and boxers and I let her push me onto the bed. I grit my teeth as warm lips immediately engulf my cock. She's barely begun and I'm already panting. I can't believe how good she is at this. I feel a sudden flash of fear as I wonder if it's because she's done this with many other men. As if she senses my sudden bout of insecurity, she pulls away from me and looks up. So many emotions are warring inside her eyes. Greed, lust, fear—but over them all is desperation. I feel ashamed for doubting her. What we have is special and unique, and I know that I am the only person who has ever seen this side of her.

She moves forward to take me in her mouth again, but I stop her. I'm too close tonight. I push her over to the window and proceed to the second part of our evening. I open the window and Alexis leans out of it. She is such a little exhibitionist. Even though our room faces a dark and deserted parking lot, the fact that someone could see us drives her wild. I pull her skirts up around her waist and slide her lace panties down her legs. She bends over just a bit more for me. I reach in her purse and find the bottle of lubricant I knew she would have. I wonder if she ever "accidentally" lets it drop out of her bag while she is in public. I bet she does.

I massage the warm globes of her ass until I feel a bit of the tension leave her body. When she leans forward even more, I slide one lubricated finger up to her tight entrance. She shivers as I slide the finger inside her. It's only a few seconds before she nods and I slide a second finger in. I wonder what all those jealous men at the restaurant would think if they knew the angel they were admiring earlier was now bent over and waiting for my cock to claim her ass. She whimpers a bit and I realize that my other hand has tightened on her narrow hips. I can feel her legs start to shake as she grips the windowsill tightly.

I stand back up and scissor my fingers inside of her. She moans and nods her head at me eagerly. She is as ready for this as I am.

Impatiently, I slick my cock with lube and then slide inside of her. The wood of the windowsill creaks under her clenched fists. I enter her slowly and savor the way her body adjusts to mine. Sweat rolls down my face and I attempt to shake my hair out of my eyes. Finally. We both let out a sigh as I push myself all the way in.

"You're so perfect, Alexis."

My hands are probably going to leave bruises on her hips, but I don't care. Christ, she always feels like heaven. I push in and pull out of her, moving in time to her heavy breathing. As she starts panting harder, I increase my thrusts until I'm slamming into her so hard she can barely breathe at all. "You are so lovely, it hurts me to look at you." The gentle words coming out of my mouth are a complete contrast to the furious pounding of our bodies, but that's how she likes it. Sweet gentle words and fast rough action. No wonder I love her.

She shifts her body, and I see that she's stroking herself. Her other arm is shaking from the strain of holding herself up now. I reach forward to replace her hand with my own. She makes a sound of appreciation and returns her hand to the window. I stroke her in time with my thrusts, and I gasp when she purposefully clenches her cheeks. She's so fucking tight. Suddenly I hit that perfect spot and she shudders against me. I grin and slide in and out rapidly, pressing against it again and again.

"Don't fucking stop! Jesus!" She throws her hips back against me with a surprising amount of strength.

"Better be careful," I gasp against her damp hair. "Somebody might hear you."

That's all it takes.

She thrusts against me violently and then stiffens. I continue to stroke her as she climaxes, and feeling that hot wetness against my hand is just what I needed.

"Oh, sweetheart…" The term slips out of my mouth unintentionally as I empty myself into her. My sweat-slick hands slip off her hips and I lean my forehead against her back as I slowly stop thrusting.

She must be feeling kind tonight. She lets me hold her for a minute. Then too quickly she leaves my arms and enters the small bathroom. She throws a towel at me and then shuts the door, locking it behind her. The sound of the lock turning echoes in my head.

I sigh and grab the water bottle out of her purse. I sit down on the unused bed and take a sip to try to relieve some of the dryness in my throat. It doesn't seem to help. I pour a little on the towel and clean myself up, trying not to think too much about what just happened. It's always the same.

I turn the TV on and flick through channels without really looking at them. I pause on a commercial for flowers and feel a small smile creep up on me. I've never brought her flowers. I'm not sure how she'd react.

I hear the bathroom door open.

My girlfriend is gone.

Instead, Alex stands there avoiding my gaze as he does after every such evening. The soft curls are gone; instead his hair is pulled back into the tight ponytail he normally sports. His eyes are hidden by a pair of reading glasses. The choker that previously covered his Adam's apple has been stuffed into the pocket of his slacks. The dress is probably hanging inside a garment bag in the bathroom. He finishes buttoning the top of his dress shirt and I stare at his hands. Hands a bit too calloused, a shade too manly. When he's Alexis, he has to hide them under gloves.

I look at my friend Alex and feel the same sense of wry amusement I always do at the end of our trysts. He's slender and his facial features are quite delicate for a man. Still, without the makeup, without the feminine clothes and accessories, nobody would ever guess that the serious young man in front of me was a blushing China doll only half an hour ago.

I long to touch him, to whisper that I need him, but I know I can't. I'm only allowed to do those things while he is Alexis. After the sex, he turns back into my childhood friend. And friends don't touch each other that way. Friends don't give each other mind-blowing orgasms and whisper sweet nothings into each other's ears. I clench my jaw and realize that I've been twisting the sheet in my fist.

He clears his throat, and I look up.

"I'll see you around. Don't forget that Susan is having everyone over for dinner on Tuesday." His voice is lower than before and holds none of the lust it did while he was Alexis.

"Don't worry; I put it on my calendar." My voice comes out strained and I hate that he is able to turn off his emotions so easily.

I don't know why he feels that he can only be intimate when he is dressed like a woman. It drives me insane. Looking at him every day, talking as though we are nothing but good buddies. Watching him flirt with girls at parties, knowing I'm the only person who knows which way he really swings. He's so fucked up.

I love him, and I can't let him know.

But as I watch him walk out the door without a backward glance I realize something. I'm just as fucked up as he is. Because even though it breaks my heart every time he leaves like that I'll keep answering his phone calls. Because I've become addicted to his alabaster skin and I can't go back.

ALISON TYLER

ABOVE YOU

ADAM AND I FIND EACH OTHER at a convention. He likes me from the start because I pay no attention to him. None at all. I don't notice him when I walk by his booth. I don't make eye contact with him from my stool in the dimly lit hotel bar. I am not playing favorites. I never pay attention to potential bedmates at the trade shows. Not because there aren't any attractive possibilities, but because I have zero desire to hook up for three days with some total stranger and then spend the next ten years at these dreary conventions in a practiced study of avoidance.

But Adam is different.

He searches me out, and he tells me things that men in L.A. don't bother saying. At least, not to me. He says that I'm unlike anyone he knows (in Erie, Pennsylvania). With his arm around my waist and his head bent low to my ear, he whispers that I've got a quality, a mystery, an aura. From the moment he saw me, arranging the books in our booth, he knew he had to meet me.

"You're different," he says, and the pull of his accent makes him suddenly sexy. "I don't know anyone like you."

It's as if he's never seen a girl with dyed black hair before. Never seen pale skin or dark eyes, all of the things that make me an aberration in Hollywood, where blonde and blue are the only colors in the crayon box. But I've seen people like Adam before. Tall, lean, and handsome in a hick sort of way. He's probably very suave (in Erie, Pennsylvania), but a little bit more earnest than the type I go for. Read between the lines: I'm just like Adam. I yearn for the ones who ignore me.

Adam says that he loves me.

And he says it even before I go down on him in the elevator.

When I meet Adam's girlfriend at the trade show the following spring, I'm surprised by how much we look alike. We are both petite, fair-skinned brunettes. I've got an inch or two on her and she's got about ten pounds on me. As we size each other up, I believe we come to the exact same conclusion: I am slightly prettier, a bit hipper, and much happier than Sarah is. The first two items on the list could be taken care of in a single afternoon. What she needs most is a good haircut and a much better dress. She could use a tattoo, or a hidden piercing, something to make her feel funky and confident, that the rest of the world doesn't know about. The happier aspect is more difficult to work with. I think that it's got nothing to do with me and everything to do with Adam.

Winning at the attractiveness game gives me an odd upper hand. An air of queendom, like when you're five years old and it's your birthday party and you get to boss other people around all day long. Sure, it's fun, but after everyone leaves, you feel sort of sick to your stomach.

As if she enjoys wallowing, Sarah befriends me. She drinks too much and puts her head on my shoulder. I feel her soft hair against my neck, her breath on my cheek when she speaks. "You're so nice," she slurs, "that's what Adam told me."

I wonder what else he told her. I've had crushes before, have gone loopy and started confessing unusual factoids about a person I liked to the one I was currently with. Did Adam talk that way about me? Or did he describe the way it felt to press me up against the elevator door, to ride me as the car traveled all the way up to the thirty-second floor?

My obvious queenliness draws other men to me while Sarah is ignored. The scruffy musician at the bar dedicates his set to the raven-haired beauty, and he nods in my direction. The waiter at our table brings me a round of free drinks. And then, of course, there's Adam.

Adam. Adam. Adam.

His foot meets mine under the table. His fingertips linger when he hands me a fresh drink. Long glances over Sarah's head make me feel as if he's not only mentally undressing me, but mentally bending me over the shaky table and fucking me doggy-style. Poor Sarah pretends that everything is normal, and I do my best to pretend along with her. Until I get too drunk to care.

Adam's brother lives in town, and when we meet him late in the evening at a club, an even more bizarre scene is waiting to unfold. Mark and Adam have their own competition going on, and when Mark sees that Adam likes me…then Mark likes me. And then suddenly it's Mark.

Mark. Mark. Mark.

Mark is married with a two-year-old daughter named Lucy. He isn't as handsome as Adam, but he's cooler in a nerdy, Buddy Holly sort of way. He knows stuff about music, and he's not just feeding me a line when he says that he's into hip-hop. He really is. We stay at the club in Baltimore until two in the morning and I dance the whole set with Mark. No cabs come to pick us up and we end up walking nearly two miles back to the hotel. Mark walks next to me, and Adam insists on walking right behind us, listening in on our conversation. Mark torments his younger brother, asking me sexy questions, making Adam jealous. And because Adam's jealous, I sense that Sarah wants to crawl into a hole in the sidewalk and die.

"I'll bet you're not wearing any panties," Mark says, just loud enough for Adam and Sarah to hear. I don't answer because I don't have to. Three sex-hungry people are now picturing me without panties. It doesn't matter whether I have them on or not. To Mark and Adam and Sarah, I am totally naked beneath my skirt. But I'm picturing Sarah's panties. I know she's wearing them, and I'm sure that they are plain, white, and cotton.

At the hotel, Mark offers to come upstairs with me while Adam leads an extremely intoxicated Sarah back to her room. She shoots me a look over her shoulder that I read as saying *I won*. Her drunken smile is lopsided and she winks.

"Be right back," Adam says. "Just going to tuck her in."

He does it, I know, because deep down he loves her. Not me. I am a fantasy creature flown in from L.A. to solve his problems and star in his daydreams. She is the woman he ought to be with.

"And I'll tuck *you* in," Mark says with a sly smile.

"You're married."

"That's my problem."

"Mine, too," I say and leave him before he can grab me and hold me back. I don't want him. I want Adam, and even though I shouldn't be, I'm surprised when he doesn't come to my room, when he doesn't even ring after putting Sarah to bed. That is, at first I'm surprised. Then I get mad. Finally, I get an idea. Although not as drunk as the rest of them, I feel my liquor as I reach for the phone. No answer at Adam's room, so I try Sarah's, not sure how I'm going to behave as she answers the phone. Turns out I don't have to worry about anything. She says simply, "I was about to call you. Come on over."

"Over" means up two floors to her room. Maybe she wants to talk. To ask me questions. To dish Adam. I don't feel like being alone, so I grab my key and ride the elevator to her floor, thinking of my ride with Adam six months earlier.

Sarah opens the door naked. I see her clothes in a mess on the floor by the bed and realize that I was wrong. Not plain white underwear, but a pair of racy black panties. High-cut on the hips. Panties I'd wear myself. Slowly, I start to reconsider the situation.

"I was just having a drink," Sarah says, shutting the door behind me and then walking across the room toward the balcony. Her haughty ass is a pleasure to watch, and I stare openly, considering my next move. I still feel the alcohol buzzing through my system, but that simply makes it easier for me to get naked myself and walk after her. It seems only fair for us to be at the same starting point. But even when

I'm without clothes, I sense that she's leading. Our roles of the evening have changed. This is her game.

Sarah hoists herself up so that she's sitting on the cold concrete wall that rims the tiny area. That makes me nervous, but she doesn't seem frightened at all. Behind her, the sky begins to lighten, still a deep blue, but no longer cobalt. Toward the east it gradually turns a faded denim color, like worn jeans.

"Look at me," Sarah says softly, bringing my attention from the sky back to her face. I see suddenly that she's very pretty. That she is different from me; it's only the surface parts that are similar.

"Do you love him?" Sarah asks.

I shrug and shake my head at the same time, spending several moments drinking in her features. She has freckles, which I hadn't noticed before. In the lights from the city, her skin takes on a golden glow, as if she'd been covered with sparkling confetti.

"Did you do it?" she asks next.

"What?" I murmur.

"Fuck. Did you fuck?"

It sounds harsh coming from her lips, and I squint at the way she says the word, then nod.

"Would you fuck me?"

I realize that I have misread her cues all evening long. Sarah wasn't playing the part of the left-out girlfriend, she was flirting with me. Her head on my shoulder. Her sweet compliments. The dirty looks she shot Adam whenever he made a forward move. While I was concocting a soap opera catfight over a guy, Sarah was letting me know that I'd turned her on. Thoughts of Adam slip away. Now, I want to play connect the dots of Sarah's freckles with my tongue, start at a freckle on her chin and work down her neck, over her breasts, along the flat of her belly, to her cunt. I also don't want her to fall off the railing, so I pull her down and then spin her around, so that she can look out at the slowly waking city while I work.

Of course, it isn't really work. The feel of her soft skin under my fingertips, under my tongue, is the ultimate pleasure. I lean up against her, so that she can feel my skin on hers, and then I press my lips to the back of her neck and lick her, then bite her. She shivers against me, and makes a soft sighing noise to let me know she likes it.

Different lovers bring out different sides of your personality. Somewhere deep inside me, I know this. Adam put me in the role of the lady, a damsel, but it takes making love to Sarah to remind me that I have a range of facets. That I can be passive with one lover and dominant with another. And I am dominant with Sarah. I play her, sliding my hands up her arms, locking her wrists together in one hand as I bend to bite the nape of her neck the way a mama cat does when it lifts a kitten. Sarah coos and I bite harder, now releasing her wrists and using one hand to spank her ass.

The predawn air flows over our naked skin, and this makes it even more spectacular as I work my way down her body, licking along the ridge of her spine, until I find the indents above her bottom. I kiss her here, waiting, forcing myself to take my time until she arches her back. Letting me know with that single move what she wants. And what she wants is exactly what I want. My tongue in her asshole. The warmth of it, the length of it. Pressing in and pulling out while she grips on to the concrete barrier and faces into the morning sky, as still as one of the gargoyles on the roof above us.

I do just as we both hoped I would, parting the cheeks of her ass, introducing her to the wetness of my tongue. I trick it in a circle around her hole before plunging inside. She makes that cooing noise again, like one of the doves on the window ledges in the room next to us. I adore that noise, want to hear it again, and I continue with my actions. Feeling her inside with my tongue, bringing one hand up the split of her body in front and tweaking her clit between my fingers. I want to make her scream, want to take her to places she's only been in her mind.

As the sky continues to lighten, I work her, fucking her with my tongue and fingers. When I sense that she's close to coming, I don't stop. I won't stop. I use both hands to spread apart her pussy lips, and then drag my thumbs over her clit, my tongue still in her ass. Anyone can eat pussy, but it takes a truly special lover to focus like this, to make a girl climax with a tongue in her hole. To do the things to your partner that you'd most like someone to do to you. I do everything to Sarah that I like the best. I take my time, which is always important, and I bring her repeatedly to the edge of climax without letting her reach it.

You never want your lover to get there too soon. Yes, it will feel good. Nobody has ever had a "bad" orgasm. But the best ones are those that you can almost taste in your mouth before they wash through your body. This is the kind I bring to Sarah, finally touching her exactly like she wants, like she needs. Varying the intensity until her whole body tenses and she screams. The contractions rage through her, slamming through her body and leaving her both satisfied and drained. She pulls away from me and turns around, staring down at me with a look of total satisfaction in her lovely eyes. I don't have to ask her how it was, and she doesn't have to tell me. But she whispers one word, "Perfect," and smiles.

In the morning, I stop by Adam's hotel room to say good-bye.

"I love you," Adam says softly. This time, there's no oral sex involved. Just Adam, looking almost tearful as he stares at me from the rumpled mess of his white bedsheets. "I love you."

And that's the last I ever hear of him.

"Maybe he didn't say that," Sarah suggests when I tell her the story afterward on our flight to L.A.

"What do you mean?" I ask, looking over at my new girlfriend. She couldn't be more different from Adam. She talks straight, doesn't play games, and would never let a lover come between her and her brother.

"Maybe you misheard him."

"Love…shove…dove…"

"Above," she says with finality. "Maybe he said, 'I'm above you.' " She pauses, considering the situation. "Was he?"

"Was he what?"

"Above you?"

I picture Adam's long lean body sprawled among the wrinkled white sheets. In my head, I can still hear him whispering the words. "I love you." That's what he said. No doubt about it. But that statement becomes our private joke forever. When Sarah wants to kiss me, to touch me, to fuck me, she leans in close and says, "I'm above you."

She's not. We are on the exact same level.

Which, I might add, is way the fuck above Adam.

ABOUT THE EDITOR

C ALLED "A TROLLOP WITH A LAPTOP" by *East Bay Express*, Alison Tyler is naughty and she knows it. Ms. Tyler is the author of more than twenty explicit novels, including *Learning to Love It*, *Strictly Confidential*, *Sweet Thing*, *Sticky Fingers*, and *Something About Workmen* (all published by Black Lace), as well as *Rumors*, *Tiffany Twisted*, and *With or Without You* (Cheek). Her novels and short stories have been translated into Japanese, Dutch, German, Italian, Norwegian, and Spanish.

Ms. Tyler's short stories in multiple genres have appeared in many anthologies as well as in *Playgirl* magazine and *Penthouse Variations*.

She is the editor of *Batteries Not Included* (Diva); *Heat Wave, Best Bondage Erotica* volumes 1 & 2, *The Merry XXXmas Book of Erotica*, *Luscious*, *Red Hot Erotica*, *Slave to Love*, *Three-Way*, *Happy Birthday Erotica*, *Caught Looking* (with Rachel Kramer Bussel), and *Got a Minute?* (all from Cleis Press); *Naughty Fairy Tales from A to Z* (Plume); and the *Naughty Stories from A to Z* series, the *Down & Dirty* series, *Naked*

Erotica, and *Juicy Erotica* (all from Pretty Things Press). Please visit www.prettythingspress.com or www.alisontyler.blogspot.com.

Ms. Tyler is loyal to coffee (black), lipstick (red), and tequila (straight). She has tattoos, but no piercings; a wicked tongue, but a quick smile; and bittersweet memories, but no regrets.

In all things important, she remains faithful to her partner of eleven years, but she still can't choose just one perfume.